Paws in the ~~~~~

A Jaz and Luffy Cozy Mystery

Book 1

Max Parrott

Copyright © 2020 Max Parrott

All rights reserved.

No part of this book may be reproduced in any form or by an electronic or mechanical means, including information storage and retrieval systems, without written permission from the author, except for the use of brief quotations in a book review.

CONTENTS

Chapter 1	1
Chapter 2	10
Chapter 3	19
Chapter 4	26
Chapter 5	37
Chapter 6	49
Chapter 7	67
Chapter 8	83
Chapter 9	97
Chapter 10	110
Chapter 11	121
Chapter 12	134
Chapter 13	148
Chapter 14	156

CHAPTER 1

The town of Blackwood Cove was hard to find on any map, due both to its small size and the remoteness of its location.

Positioned along a stretch of the New England coastline not often seen by anyone but the hardiest of fishermen, the Cove, as the locals called it, was nestled up tight between two rugged and forbidding cliffs. Even if you happened to pass by it on your oceanic travels, you might be hard-pressed to distinguish many details, for the town was shrouded almost continually in a cold, clammy blanket of sea fog. Even at the height of summer, the Cove rarely saw temperatures in excess of seventy-five degrees. And in winter, the residents often joked they were trapped inside a snow globe. Trapped, with no way out.

There was only one road in and out of the Cove. A two lane stretch of asphalt, crumbling from the endless cycle of frost and thaw, meandered in curving switchbacks up the relatively gentle slope behind the town. It then became lost in dense and shadowed forest, stretching for over fifteen miles before it reached the next settlement.

Nearly a hundred years ago, Blackwood Cove had been an important fishing and shipping location. However, as the coastline further south was built up and added onto, the Cove became less and less vital. Now it made most of its money either through tourism or the generous contributions of wealthy, older folk who had decided to make it their very own retirement community.

Home to over two thousand at its peak, Blackwood Cove was now host to a mere eight hundred and fifty souls, as its oft-edited welcome sign announced. It was a strange sight for the traveler to behold as they came coasting down out of that primeval and seemingly endless forest. A scattering of ancient buildings set in terraces that sloped toward a gray and dismal beach, fog curling through the streets, filling the empty paths where once a never-ending stream of shoppers had strolled.

It was currently autumn in the Cove. Winter was just around the corner. The few deciduous trees around the town, including the ancient oak on the town commons, had lost all but a few black, curling leaves. The evergreens stood tall and proud, ready to accept their tonnage of winter snow. It wouldn't be long, no more than a couple of weeks, before the town of Blackwood Cove entered the long slumber. Short days and long nights. Frosted window panes and screaming sea winds, driving frigid air beneath their doors.

But for now, there was still a little bit of life left in the place. The local school, a building the size of the average middle school in a larger town, housed every grade from preschool on up. As the clock wore on toward the afternoon, less than a hundred students stared out the windows and urged time to move faster.

In the sleepy residential streets across town, along the populated stretches past the boarded-up homes of long-gone people, nothing much was happening. A cat ran across Ivy Road, pausing halfway along to glance toward a slow oncoming car with its ears erect and its eyes wide open. It then continued on its journey, toward home or toward some hunting grounds, and vanished along the brick foundation of an abandoned house.

A child, too young to be in school, was pedaling a tricycle along at a painstaking speed on the sidewalk of Foghorn Drive. The boy's mother walked along behind, smiling and laughing even as her cheeks turned red in the bracing air.

And on Main Street, under the glow of a half dozen OPEN signs, a trio of old women were walking along. Bundled up in their cold weather gear, they set their sights on the next shopping destination. And further ahead of them, where the street widened into a broad cul-de-sac, stood the town commons. A library, the oldest building in the Cove, held council over the broad and windswept grounds. Near to that was a town hall, barely more than a tool shed in size, as well as the large manor where the mayor lived with his wife.

Down by the seashore, bouncing along on the brackish waves in the small harbor, there was an expensive-looking pleasure craft. It stood out like a sore thumb from the more conservative boats around it, including a mossy old canoe that had been tied up there for almost two decades, never having been claimed or used by anyone.

And, standing outside her parent's home on silent Temple Street on the northeastern fringe of the town, a young woman named Jasmine Moore was contemplating the future.

At nineteen years of age, it seemed like an entire universe of possibilities was open to her. But the longer she stayed here, on the misty boulevards of her home town, the more content she felt just to wallow forever in the familiarity of it all. Yet, she couldn't help but feel there was a greater destiny waiting for her. It was a paradox of feeling that every human being had felt at one time or another... though Jasmine, being young, naturally felt like she was the only person in the world who was dealing with it.

But this feeling came from a place of logic. After all, she knew for a fact that she was unique in at least one way.

"What are we waiting for?" a gruff, friendly voice asked from somewhere near her right knee.

She glanced down and saw Luffy there, using his back right paw to get at an itch behind his ear. He put his foot down and looked up at her with wide, brown eyes. Eyes that were excited, but not expectant. Eager, but patient.

"Well," Jasmine said with a smile, patting him on the head, "it's only 12:41."

"So?" Luffy asked, cocking his head.

"So," Jasmine added, "it only takes me fifteen minutes to get to the Nook. There's no reason to leave until quarter to one."

"There's nothing wrong with being early," Luffy pointed out.

"And there's nothing wrong with being exactly on time!" she replied. "Don't try and push me, mister. I know your angle. You think if we set off early, we'll be able to do a lap around the commons."

"Walking is fun," said Luffy.

"Walking. Right."

He cocked his head again. "What do you mean?"

Jasmine laughed. "We both know all you want to do is pee on that big old oak tree."

"It smelled wrong the last time we were there," Luffy replied in a defensive tone. "I still have that smell stuck in my nose. I need to get rid of it."

"Well, we'll swing by after my shift. How does that sound?"

Luffy barked once, wagging his tail to show that her suggestion was perfectly fine by him.

And then they waited. In the silence, as a foghorn blared somewhere out at sea and echoed eerily through the town, Jasmine experienced a moment of realization. It was not normal, by any definition of the word, to be able to talk to your dog. Sure, every dog knew a few words in the language of their human masters. Walk, food, bath, dish, et cetera. Speak, shake, sit, roll over. Play dead. But what she and Luffy had went far beyond that. And it was only with him. She could talk to Luffy, and Luffy could talk to her... but she had no such connection with any other canine.

When she was younger, when she first found Luffy stranded on the beach, she had thought she was a freak. Some kind of mutated creature that would never fit in to society. Sometimes she still felt that way, like she wasn't quite human. These thoughts were the only thing she ever hid from Luffy. He was the innocent party in all this. He was nothing but a faithful friend, a confidant, someone who was always there for her. He did not deserve her burdens, as much as she knew he would carry them gladly if only to save her a shred of pain.

"Okay," she said, glancing at her watch. "Let's go."

Luffy pranced along behind her, bouncing excitedly. He knew the way. He could run there on his own with a blindfold on. But he knew the rules. It was a two-way bargain. He didn't need to wear a leash, as long as he stayed close and let her lead.

"It's a nice day," Luffy remarked, sniffing at her hand.

"Yeah, real nice," she replied sarcastically. "Forty-nine degrees. Wind blowing at about, I dunno, twelve miles an hour. Pretty much the perfect conditions for sailing, come to think of it."

"I bet Mrs. Carter will be going out onto the water today. Maybe we can tag along. I love sailing. I love it!"

"Sure thing, Luffy. We'll just walk right up to the mayor's wife and ask if she wouldn't mind us tagging along on her latest expedition. I'm sure she'd love to host the weird dog girl and her pet for a day."

"What do you mean? I'm sure she thinks we're cool," Luffy said.

"I doubt it. She likes Barry, remember?"

That took the wind out of Luffy's sails, so to speak. At the mention of Barry Brock's name, he growled deep in his throat.

"Down, boy," Jasmine said. "We're not going to hurt Barry. Right?"

"Right," Luffy agreed. "I love people. Most of them."

The rest of the walk passed in silence. Luffy moved out a foot to her right, sniffing grass in every lawn they passed. When it was time to cross a street, he tucked in by her side again for a brief moment. Not that there was much need. This time of day, the Cove was silent and dead. They might as well have been the last two remaining residents in a ghost town.

***

The Book Nook proudly claimed, according to a hand carved wooden sign in the front window, to be BLACKWOOD COVE'S PREMIER BOOKSHOP. Though the sign looked new, having been maintained and retouched on an annual basis by the proprietor, it was actually nearly as old as the store itself. And it told a long story of competition with another store which used to occupy a boarded-up husk standing at the other end of Main Street.

The Nook itself laid claim to one of the oldest and most elegantly decorated store fronts in the entire commercial district of Blackwood Cove... and as dubiously impressive a claim as that was, the owner took it very seriously. The red bricks of the facade were re-pointed once a year. Cultivated ivy was allowed to grow on some of it, having been shaped and culled into a desirable curtain shape. The ancient windows, paned with glass that was foggier than the average morning in the Cove, let out streams of warm, amber light and smeared visions of stacked books and cozy ambiance.

It was easily Jasmine's favorite place in the entire world. Even before she had been lucky enough to get a job there, she spent many hours of her life lost in those wonderful stacks of books, basking in the rich smells of old pages, reveling in the knowledge that endless stories stood all around her, just waiting to be discovered.

Having made good time on her walk over, courtesy of a strong wind at her back, Jasmine stepped inside the shop at 12:58. Her feet fell on oak planks that were older than her father, squeaking as her weight settled on them. She wiped her feet on a nearby rug and then stepped in past the vestibule, into a narrow alleyway between shelves of books that had once been double stacked but were now triple stacked, overflowing with volumes. At last count, another activity which the proprietor performed obsessively, the Nook had been home to over ten thousand books. Impressive, considering its cramped size.

Jasmine looked around for a long moment, taking a deep breath and steeping in it all. Like a tea bag sinking to the bottom of a cup and luxuriating in the rich depths. New books were well and good. Sometimes you had to read them if it was something that had just come out. But to Jasmine's mind, there was nothing more magical than a room jammed floor to ceiling with dog-eared treasures, cracked spines, and yellowed pages. Even the occasional staining or mold growth or mysterious sticky object between two pages could not dissuade her in her love for used books.

"Jaz, is that you?" a voice called from somewhere in the teetering maze walls of the book shop.

"Yes, Patrick," she called back. "I'm just hanging up my coat."

"Well, join me back here once you're done."

Luffy padded along behind her as she navigated the narrow aisles. She found Patrick Walker in the science fiction and fantasy section, on his knees with bags of books positioned around him.

"That neighbor of yours just dumped off another truckload," he grunted. "I guess she thinks we're running the Library of Congress here. Like we've got unlimited space! Here, help me shove some of these down..."

He seemed to be trying to insert books into an empty space on the shelf. However, the unsupported books to either side kept trying to tip over and fill in that space. Jaz pulled them aside and held them in place while he inserted a pre-sorted stack of volumes.

"That does it," he said. "Look at that. It's a whole series. *Almost.* We've got books one through five now. Except there's *six* in all. It's not like the last book didn't come out yet. It was published in '89, for Pete's sake! What's she doing, holding onto it for a rainy day?"

"'89, huh?" Jasmine asked. "How did you know that?"

"Well..." Patrick looked up at her with an almost shameful look on his face. "I'm getting old now, Jaz. My eyes aren't what they used to be. Heck, neither is the rest of me. And we've got more books than we've ever had before. So, I finally let that Watson kid help me out with getting the internet hooked up. You know, that no-good coworker of yours. And I guess it isn't so bad. There's a lot of information out there."

"Did he say internet?" Luffy asked.

"I can't believe it," Jasmine replied, grinning and gently knocking her boss on the shoulder. "I guess you can teach an old dog new tricks."

"You're not talking about me, are you?" Luffy asked.

"To use the old cliché, I guess you can," said Patrick. "Teach an old dog new tricks. I wonder how many of the books in this place have that same line in them? Maybe you need to get some new material, Jaz."

He stood up, lifting an old hardcover from the top shelf. It was at the front, which meant he had only just stocked it. The corners were dented in and the spine seemed to have scoliosis, it was so crooked. It was beautiful.

"You see this?" Patrick asked. "I read this book when I was just a kid. I forgot it even existed at all before your neighbor brought it in. Funny how life is, sometimes."

"Yeah," Jasmine said. "Funny."

Patrick stared at the book for a long time, his eyes going distant. Finally, he slid it onto the shelf and let out a sigh.

"Well," he said, "I guess I've got you for the next four hours, so I might as well put you to work. Would you rather stock shelves or tend the register?"

She knew how he got about his shelves. If someone else did them, Patrick would always end up *re*doing them.

"The register's fine," she said. "Luffy can keep me company. Right, boy?"

"Jeez, Jasmine," Luffy replied. "You don't have to talk to me like I'm a dog."

***

While the nook was certainly receiving more trade-ins than ever before, it was far less profitable than it might have seemed. For one thing, the increasing number of books was an indicator that people were buying less. Though Patrick Walker outwardly acted as though nothing was wrong, he had nevertheless been a ball of nervous energy for the weeks and months leading up to this fateful week.

Jasmine Moore, Jaz as most in the Cove called her, was aware of none of this. She whiled away her shift at the counter, reading and talking quietly with Luffy in between customers. She enjoyed a soda from the mini fridge under the counter, daydreaming as time passed by.

And time did pass, faster than anyone in Blackwood Cove ever could have expected. It was winding down, drawing toward the last moment of peace the town would know for quite some time.

Because someone out of that population of eight hundred and fifty was about to come up dead.

CHAPTER 2

Jaz was aware of a slight change in the mood about town as she exited the bookstore, turning the sign to the CLOSED position behind her. As she waited for Patrick to lock the door, she looked up and down Main Street. Usually there would be at least a dozen or so folks visible just then, headed into the Chop House for their dinner, or the Leaky Trawler for a drink. However, there was no one around. No one but ghosts, and the fog that crept in from the sea. Maybe everyone knew something she didn't, or they just felt that something wasn't right.

"Where is everyone?" Luffy asked.

Glancing at Patrick, Jasmine simply shrugged in reply.

"Alright," Patrick said, shoving his keys into his pocket. "Another day, done and dusted. Thanks for your help, Jaz."

She smiled. "Not a problem, Mr. Walker. I'm just doing my job. Literally. You know you pay me for this, right?"

"Um... let me check with my accountant," Patrick replied with a grin. "Of course I know that, Jaz. But I feel I don't need to. All the free books seem like compensation enough. See you tomorrow, then."

"No, that's Brandon's shift."

"Oh," said Patrick. "Well, that little jerk can take another look at my computer. I think he's managed to put a virus on it."

"Or maybe it's the fact that you've had the same machine for twelve years," Jasmine suggested.

Patrick shrugged. "Nah. That can't be it. Goodnight then, Jaz.

And you too, Luffy."

He stooped down, giving the dog a nice scratch behind the ears. Luffy ate it up, his tail wagging the entire time. And then Patrick was gone, strolling back up Main Street toward the town commons. In a moment he would turn right down Maple and head home. There was, according to him, one major benefit to living in such a small town; cars were unnecessary. Walking could get you everywhere.

Unless, of course, your destination was out at sea.

Turning away from The Book Nook, Jasmine made her way back through a downtown that was even sleepier than usual. Just about every shop was already closed at this hour. The flower place, the salon, the tiny little antiques store, the bakery. All were dark and locked up, the windows shuttered. The street was quiet as the girl and her dog walked along it, wordless and waiting expectantly. Because the air was charged with that sort of feeling; the feeling that something was about to happen.

"I think we can skip our lap around the commons," Luffy said.

"Aw, shucks," Jasmine said with mock sympathy. "Why do you say that?"

"I'm getting the creeps out here. You feel it too. I can tell. Dogs are very perceptive, and you humans aren't as good at hiding your feelings as you think."

Jasmine nodded. "Well... it does feel a little weird out here. It almost feels like it should be Halloween night."

"That's not until *next* week, but I get what you're saying," Luffy said with a humorous lilt to his voice. Then, he suddenly nudged his nose into her hand and said in a concerned tone, "Jasmine, you need to sit down. It's about to happen again."

His words made her heart skip a beat. She stopped dead in her tracks, looking both ways up and down Main Street. Making sure she wasn't witnessed. Then she quickly strode to the steps of the barbershop and plopped down on them. The cement was cold and hard beneath her. It anchored her in reality as she began to breathe deeply, grasping Luffy with both hands for comfort, digging her fingers into his fur.

Then, it came.

With a sigh, Jasmine sank against the glass door behind her. She began to twitch now and then, as though dreaming, but she was aware of none of this. She was somewhere else.

Luffy sat there upon the steps, his tongue hanging out as he breathed out plumes of frost. He watched his human closely, occasionally bringing his nose close to her face to smell her breath.

Finally, Jasmine coughed and choked and sat forward, beating herself in the chest to regulate her breathing. She hugged Luffy to her, narrowing her eyes as he licked her face.

"Are you OK?" he asked.

"Fine," she said. "It was just like the other times."

"I don't like this, Jasmine. This isn't like you and I being able to talk. That's a natural thing. A bond we share. This is something else."

Jasmine nodded, feeling numb. It was only the third such episode she had ever experienced. The first had occurred over a month ago. The second had happened just last week. And now... It seemed they were getting more frequent. She was terrified that they might start happening every day. Maybe more than once.

And they weren't just seizures.

"What did you see this time?" Luffy asked.

"I... don't know," Jasmine stammered, rubbing her temples. "Wait. Okay. It's getting clear now. Sorry, it's like a dream. Sometimes you remember a lot of details, sometimes you don't."

"Not sure why you're apologizing," Luffy grunted.

"It was a cottage," she went on. "It was Jack's place."

"Jack Torres?" Luffy asked. "Crazy Jack? That's the only house in town I don't dare walk up to. And not just because he has a mean cat. What else did you see?"

"I was there," said Jasmine. "But I kind of wasn't. I was just floating along, like I was seeing everything in a movie. The front door was wide open. But not because of the wind. Someone had gone inside. Everything was wrong... It *felt* wrong, Luffy. Like something bad was about to happen."

Luffy, being a dog, was very sensitive to those sorts of feelings. He came closer to her, curling his head behind her neck protectively.

"Is that all?" he asked.

"No," she said, suddenly remembering. "I saw Brandon. He was there too, somewhere close by. He was sneaking along. He looked scared."

"You're remembering this one pretty clearly," Luffy pointed out.

"Only because I'm telling it to you right away," she said.

After another minute, she felt well enough to stand up and continue toward home.

***

In her room, after dinner, Jasmine pulled the old notebook out of her desk and flipped it open to a dog-eared page. There, she had written down a few minor notes about her previous visions, or hallucinations, or whatever they were.

1 - Fuzzy. Uncertain. Someone is in trouble for something they did. Their shoes are wet, leaving footprints.

2 - The grocery store is closed for the first day anyone can remember. No one in town can get any food.

Under those two short entries, she wrote a slightly more detailed account of what she had just seen. Then she put her notebook away and tried to forget everything.

"You done yet?" Luffy asked. "Because I've gotta go mark my territory."

***

This wasn't a vision, only a dream. The stacks at The Book Nook had grown and grown until they hit the ceiling. Patrick decided to raise the ceiling once, gaining an extra few feet. But when the piles grew again, he had to raise it again, and so on over and over until you couldn't even see the ceiling anymore, it was so far above your head. Lost in shadow, with impossible towers of books rising toward it. And not only had the ceiling height increased, but every other dimension in the store had extended to surreal proportions. To reach the romance section, you now had to walk two miles from the front door through a wild labyrinth where strange book-obsessed denizens lurked, waiting to jump out and...

Jasmine awoke to the sound of her alarm. She sat up with a moan. It hadn't been a very pleasant dream, but she had still been excited to see how it would end. Except dreams didn't have endings, as far as she knew.

Luffy was there when she woke. He asked her how she was feeling. Whether or not she was up to an early morning walk. She stroked his back a few times before dragging herself out of bed and glancing at the time. It was 7:03, and she had an appointment in less than half an hour.

"We'll need to walk to get over there," Jasmine said, rubbing her eyes. "Breakfast first."

"Breakfast!" Luffy exclaimed. "Yes, let me have it! Food is a fine substitution for walking outside! What are we eating today?"

She chuckled as she stumbled out of her bedroom and down the stairs. And this was where her conversation with Luffy ended. She could no longer treat him like anything more than a friendly canine companion. Because her parents were there, having coffee, and she hadn't told even them about what she was capable of. At first, when she discovered her gift or her curse at the age of fourteen, she feared they might send her away to some special school. And now...

Well, the answer was simple really. Secrets and lies aren't often the same thing, but they both have the same sort of inertia. They build up over time. They spread through the web of your reality like a cancerous growth, affecting everything in some way, and eventually it gets to the point where excising them from your life is nearly impossible. And that was where she was. She and her parents had a good relationship. They were proud of her for staying home and saving more money to attend a good college, rather than running off to the first cheap one that accepted her. They were happy to have her around, because without her (and Luffy, for that matter) they would enter empty nest syndrome instantaneously.

There was no reason to bring up something they might accuse her of lying about, or else insist she see a doctor for. She knew she wasn't crazy, but she also knew there was no hope of convincing anyone else of that.

Not anyone but Luffy. He was her best friend, and so of course he received a few table scraps on the sly as she bolted down a quick breakfast. She was never hungry so soon after waking, but she made herself eat.

"Big day planned?" her father asked. Peter Moore was a successful businessman who worked in the next town over. He had already finished his food and had graduated to the coffee sipping, newspaper reading, glancing-at-his-watch segment of the morning.

"I'm training Cynthia Jackson's poodle at 7:45," Jasmine replied. "After that I might swing by the school and see if I can help with anything. Other than that I'm not sure what else I have planned."

"No shift at the Nook?" asked her mother. Ashley Moore once worked as a secretary at the very same business where her husband was employed, but his success had allowed her to stay at home while she cared for their daughter. And she had never got around to going back.

"Not today," Jasmine replied, reaching down to scratch Luffy's ears and smuggle a small piece of bacon into his mouth. "It's Brandon's turn."

"Speaking of that boy," her father said, setting his newspaper down and fixing her with a stern gaze. "Have you told him no yet?"

Jasmine sighed and shook her head.

"Why not?" her father asked. "He doesn't intimidate you, does he?"

"No, dad!" she said with a groan. "I don't think Brandon would be able to intimidate a fly. I just don't know yet. I don't know if I want to go out with him. And I don't know if I *don't*. He's nice, but..."

"Just let him down easy," her father said, lifting his paper again. "But not too easy. Young men are fools about love. If you don't spell it out explicitly, they'll always think they still have a chance."

Ashley Moore smiled as she scrawled in another word on her crossword puzzle. "Don't always believe your father, Jasmine. If he had listened to his own advice when we were young, you never would have been born."

"You only turned me down twice, woman," Peter replied. "As they say, third time's the charm. You can't blame a guy for trying."

Jasmine pretended to be sick, gagging as she took another bite of toast. She washed it down with a gulp of orange juice, looked at her watch, and stood up.

"I've gotta go," she announced. "Mom, I can do the dishes when I get back."

"Not if I do them first," her mother said with a smile.

***

"Wait up!"

It was the voice she knew she would hear as soon as she stepped outside. He lived close by, and it wasn't abnormal for him to somehow find a way to be "just walking past" when Jasmine left home.

She turned around to see Brandon Watson running toward her, his pale cheeks showing tiny red spots. Those spots were always there, whether it was cold out or not.

"Wait, Jaz!" he called out again, finally catching up and kneeling to give Luffy a few pets. "I'm glad I caught you. I was wondering if you wanted to trade shifts with me. Yours tomorrow for mine today."

"Uh... why?" Jasmine asked. "Do you suddenly have something going on in your life?"

He chuckled nervously as he stood back up. "I just have some stuff I need to do today. And if I spend longer than ten minutes in the Nook, I'll probably just fall asleep."

She noticed that his eyes were red and he looked dazed.

"Didn't you sleep last night?" she asked.

"Uh... not really," he said with a groan. "I was up late."

"What were you doing?" she asked with a grin. "Chatting to girls?"

"No!" he said defensively. "I was... doing nothing, really. Nothing exciting. Well, do you want to trade or not? If you don't, that's cool."

"I can do it," Jasmine replied. "One to five, right?"

"Right!"

He stuck out his hand. She shook with him. He looked immensely relieved.

"Don't look too happy," she told him. "My shift is *noon* to five tomorrow. You'll have to spend a whole extra hour surrounded by all those wonderful, beautiful books; and that is the easiest job you'll ever have. The horror!"

"I hope Patrick won't be mad," Brandon said, cringing. "I told him I'd troubleshoot his computer today."

"Isn't that like trying to bring a dinosaur back to life by hitting the bones with a defibrillator? He just needs to admit defeat and get a new computer."

"I've tried telling him that! The guy's the most sentimental, nostalgic person I've ever met! He won't even let go of a rubber band, let alone that piece of junk computer. I tried telling him he can display it at home as museum piece, but he didn't go for it."

"I think he's just lazy, actually," Jasmine said. "He doesn't want to have to transfer any of his files over."

"Well, when the computer finally dies and he can't access any of his precious files, guess who he'll blame?" Brandon asked.

"You."

"Right! Maybe you can try and talk some sense into him today, Jaz."

"Or maybe you can stop being a pushover and request some extra money for your IT services."

"Nah," Brandon said. "The computer gives me something to do while I'm waiting for the next old lady to wander in and buy a handful of cheesy romance novels. Anyway, I've gotta go, Jaz. Did you... um... did you think about...?"

"I don't have an answer yet," she said. She decided that was succinct enough. Honest. To the point.

Brandon nodded, his posture changing. He started to shrink in on himself, as though he was trying to hide. He was a tall young man, but he managed to look like a hunchback as he slinked away, dragging his tormented heart with him.

It had never been a secret to Jasmine that Brandon had a crush on her. It went all the way back to grade school, when the quiet, shy boy did his best to always be sitting next to her, to always be with her for every group project. And there was no way it was a coincidence that Brandon, who had always been more into video games than books, had gotten hired at The Book Nook only a few weeks after her.

She wished she could tell him yes or no. But this was just the latest in a line of uncertainties that never seemed to end.

CHAPTER 3

"Okay, it's like this," Luffy said. "Teresa believes she deserves a treat every time she does a trick. But Cynthia is only giving her one if she does a trick three times in a row. That's why Teresa isn't being so obedient these days. It's really simple, Jasmine. You and I know this. If you want a loyal friend, the easiest way is to give them something tasty."

Meanwhile, Cynthia Jackson was witnessing the same thing that every one of Jasmine's clients witnessed. Jasmine stood there, appearing to be in deep thought, rubbing her chin sagely as she considered the matter at hand. In just a moment, she would say something insightful and brilliant that would solve the crisis.

"Okay, I think I know what the problem is," Jasmine finally said.

Cynthia stepped forward, listening eagerly. She had once been the most beautiful young woman in all of Blackwood Cove. And now she was the most beautiful *older* woman. Time had done nothing to diminish her looks; it had only matured them into a different form. A brand-new book with crisp pages, versus a well-worn, used book that had been read and loved and cherished for years.

"You've been asking Teresa to work for diminishing returns," Jasmine went on. "Some dogs only need the approval and joy of their owners as compensation, and they'll perform tricks all day long. But other dogs need a little more incentive. It just so happens that Teresa falls into the latter group."

"Okay, good going," Luffy said. "Use those big words. You humans love those."

Cynthia nodded, looking relieved. "Do you think I should give her more treats?"

"No," Jasmine said.

"*What?*" Luffy asked in disbelief. "And now to translate for Teresa, *what?*"

"Dogs don't always know what's best for them," Jasmine went on, talking to both dogs and to Cynthia at once. "It's up to us as their human companions to take care of them. Teresa obviously wants more treats, but that would make her obese."

"So what should I do?" Cynthia asked. "I thought I was doing the right thing, feeding her once every three tricks..."

"That could be the right thing for another dog, but not for Teresa. You should be giving her a treat for every trick. Reward her for doing what you ask, and she will fall in line."

"But you just said she would become obese!" Cynthia said.

Jasmine just smiled at her, waiting for the truth to sink in.

"Oh!" Cynthia gasped, bringing a hand to her mouth. "I see! I just ask her to do tricks less often."

"You got it," Jasmine said, firing a finger gun at her client. "That's my recommendation, anyway. You will have to try it out with Teresa and see if it works for the both of you."

The poodle barked, wagging her fluffy tail.

"Teresa seems alright with it," Luffy said, surprised. "She doesn't realize that this means she'll be getting the exact same number of treats as before. I guess not all dogs are great at math."

"Just you," Jasmine whispered, giving him a scratch.

It was then that she saw the last thing she wanted to see.

A cherry red convertible was rolling slowly down the road at the edge of the commons. As she watched it, her eyes narrowing and her bottom lip pushing out angrily, the black cloth top retracted and disappeared behind the rear seats. The car slowed to a stop nearby, and a dark-haired man in reflective aviator sunglasses waved his hand.

"How are y'all doing this morning?" he called out.

"Oh, just fine," Cynthia replied, giving him a little wave back.

Luffy growled again.

This man was Barry Brock. At forty-one years old he was set in his ways, used to being the only name in town as far as dog care and training was involved. People still came from all over the state to see him, and there was even talk that he might be getting his own TV reality show... however, none of this stopped the petulant man from getting jealous that a young woman was taking about five percent of his business. To his slight credit, that percentage *was* growing.

"I'm glad to hear it," said Brock. He then fixed his sights on the poodle, leaning out of his car and smiling. "And how are you, Teresa? Who's a good girl, huh?"

The poodle recognized her name, wagging her tail and licking her nose as her paws moved restlessly beneath her.

"Don't worry, Jasmine," Luffy said. "I'll talk some sense into the girl. Next time she sees him, she'll bite him on the nose."

"Listen," Brock said next, looking back up at Cynthia. "If you ever need someone to help you take the best possible care of your magnificent pet, you can give me a call any time. It would be my pleasure. I'll even offer a special discount, just for you."

"Yeah," said Luffy, "and he'd still charge ten times what we do. The guy's a crook."

"Oh, thank you Mr. Brock," Cynthia said politely. "But Ms. Moore and I have already been working on Teresa together."

Brock smiled, lowering the sunglasses on his nose for a moment to get a good look at Jasmine. "Oh, is that what this is? I applaud you, Ms. Jackson, for tossing a quarter to the kid's lemonade stand. It's a fine community service, what you're doing. But the town commons is no place for proper dog training. Why don't you swing by my office later on? I have extensive facilities. We can take care of Teresa the way she deserves. Well, farewell now."

He waggled his fingers as he accelerated off into the town,

turning swiftly down Main Street. That was his way. Get in, throw out a few quick digs, and get out before the opposition could formulate a rebuttal.

"What an ass," Cynthia said. "Did you hear what he said about you, Jasmine? I wouldn't take my dog to see that jerk if he was the only trainer on Earth."

That made Jasmine's heart swell, quenching her anger somewhat. "I'm glad you feel that way, Ms. Jackson. Luffy and I hate the man too."

"*Hate* him," Luffy added for emphasis.

"Unfortunately," Cynthia added, "the rest of the town seems to love him. They think he's just the most charismatic and wonderful man. Especially since he's bringing a bit more attention back to the Cove."

She shook her head, staring off into the distance.

"Is something bothering you, Ms. Jackson?" Jasmine asked.

"Oh, please," the older woman said, waving a hand. "Call me Cynthia. And yes, something *is* bothering me. But it's nothing you need to worry yourself over. If you don't mind, I'd like to set up another meeting next week so we can talk about Teresa's progress. If that's alright with you?"

"I work at The Book Nook from noon to five on Monday, Wednesday and Friday," Jasmine said. "But I'm free other than that."

"Great! How about, say, Tuesday at nine?"

"That works for me."

"And me," Luffy said. "Plenty of time for a morning walk."

***

The body was discovered at 8:19 AM that morning. It was a Thursday. The high temperature was 51 degrees, the low somewhere in the upper thirties. The sea at that time was fairly calm. There was minor tidal action, lapping softly at the gray beach. There was little wind, and the morning blanket of fog had not dissipated much. If it had, the dead man might have been spotted much earlier.

He was discovered by Randy Ballard, the manager of the

Shoppe Right grocery store. Mr. Ballard had been out on his morning walk before heading in for his long shift at nine. It was his custom to take a long lap of almost the entire town, starting at his house on Foghorn Drive, circling around the town commons and then trailing down the beach as far as he could go in both directions before the cliffs reared up and blocked him off.

He didn't see the corpse at first. It was only on his way back up into town that he happened to glance out into the surf. His eyes found a dark shape drifting there, and he immediately understood that something was wrong.

By 9:04 the local police, all three active officers, had been down to the beach. After taking notes and photographs of the entire scene, what little there was, they finally braved the cold water and dragged the body in with gloved hands. Only then did they discover the identity of the deceased.

By noon, they had a tentative time and cause of death.

***

"You've got to be kidding me!" Patrick suddenly yelled.

Jasmine finally looked up from her novel and toward the door. She was vaguely aware that someone had come in a minute or two ago, and that they and Patrick had been quietly conversing since then. Now, it seemed, there had been some kind of stunning revelation.

"Okay," Patrick said now, in the manner of a man who is trying hard to accept something that is fundamentally unacceptable. Which was to say, he blew the word out like he was trying to get a bug out of his mouth. "Thanks for stopping by, Cliff. Okay. Talk to you later."

The door closed. Through the fogged windows, Jasmine saw a vague form vanishing from sight along the sidewalk. A moment later, Patrick reappeared in view. His reading glasses were nearly falling off the end of his nose; he had closed the slim western novel he had been reading over his finger to save his place, but he looked ready to drop the book onto the floor. His face was all pursed up like he had a slice of lemon in his mouth.

"That was Cliff Adams," he said.

"I know," Jasmine said. The words came out quietly, because she couldn't seem to find much breath for speaking. It seemed the feeling of last night, of things hanging in the balance and something just about to occur, had finally come to fruition.

"Jack Torres is... dead," Patrick said in disbelief. And then, strangely, a little smile came to his features. A noise somewhat like a chuckle escaped from him. And then he brought his eyes back to Jasmine and gained swift control over himself.

"Crazy Jack," Jasmine said, her head seeming to spin.

"Good riddance," Luffy said. "But how sad. I don't like it when people die. No dog should ever outlive the humans around him."

She reached down, seizing the scruff of Luffy's neck hard. Jack Torres, the black sheep of the town who had lived alone in that tiny cottage by the sea. The very same cottage she had seen just the evening before in a vision, standing wide open, with Brandon Watson creeping somewhere nearby it...

"How?" she asked next.

"Drowning," Patrick said. "That's what the police think. They found him face down in the water near the beach. I guess he died sometime late last night, early this morning... Best as they can tell, anyway. Cliff said there's going to be a meeting outside the town hall in a couple of hours. I reckon we should close the shop down early today and walk over."

Jasmine nodded. Her mind was still reeling, and she couldn't think to ask any more questions. Though there were many she might have asked.

The next thing she knew, she and Luffy were alone again. Patrick had wandered off into the stacks somewhere. It was only two o'clock. And for the first time in the Nook's long history, as far she knew, it would close before five.

Suddenly, she realized something that made her blood run cold.

"Brandon!" she said.

"I know what you mean," Luffy replied.

"Jack was his uncle!"

"Oh," said Luffy. "Right. His uncle. Yeah."

"Oh, no," Jasmine moaned, putting her head in her hands. "I feel terrible."

"You want some advice?" Luffy asked. "Don't. Brandon doesn't care any more about that nut than anyone else around here."

"He was family," Jasmine pointed out.

"Okay, so we'll pay our respects," Luffy conceded. "Just so you know, after the funeral, the first thing I'm gonna do is pee on his gravestone. Remember that time he threw a rock at us because we got one inch too close to his cottage? It almost hit my paw!"

CHAPTER 4

By the time she was readying the store for close, counting the drawer and adding up sales versus trade-ins, her mind was starting to work again. And it was coming up with some intriguing questions.

First of all, how in the name of Poseidon could a guy like Jack Torres *drown?* He had been in his fifties. Not old by any stretch of the imagination. And he had been sailing the seas outside Blackwood Cove since he was a teenager. Maybe longer. He had the type of experience most sailors only dream of. And, thinking back, she could remember an anecdote her father had once told her.

A few years before she was born, a storm to end all storms had hit the Cove. Jack had been out on his own, looking for fish or just cruising along for pleasure, when it hit. Every last boat that was moored up at the harbor had been dashed to pieces. Waves had come in that were so high they flooded a few of the houses down on Bristol Lane, the lowest street in town but still thirty feet above sea level on a good day. It was assumed that Jack's chances of survival were basically zero.

However, hours after the storm finally moved on, a car no one had seen before rolled into town. And out stepped Jack Torres from the passenger seat with a wild story to tell. His boat had been capsized. He was on deck at the time, the only reason he hadn't gone down with it. From there on, he had half swam, half floated fifteen miles down the rocky coastline to another beach where an amateur storm chaser was filming the weather. He had done that in waves that crested thirty or forty feet. It was Jasmine's opinion that, if you put someone in a perfectly calm swimming pool and asked them to go fifteen miles without getting out and with nothing other than a tiny life vest for company, they would give up long before they made it.

But Jack couldn't give up. If his focus faltered for even a few seconds he would have died.

Granted, the man had been over two decades younger back then. And that was before he had become the heavy drinker he was these days. So she still found it difficult to believe a legendary swimmer like that could have just up and drowned in a calm ocean.

When she voiced her doubts to Patrick as they were walking out, he immediately shook his head.

"Stranger things have happened," he said quickly. "We'll probably never know how Jack ended up in whatever position he was in, but I'm sure he drowned. I'm sure it was just a terrible accident."

"Yeah," she agreed. "I'm sure."

It was a short walk to the town hall from there. Even from the front door of the Nook, they could see the crowd that had already gathered, milling around and humming with talk. A good ten percent of the Cove's population had shown. The rest were probably at home, babysitting or otherwise, waiting patiently for the other members of their house to return and tell them the situation.

Jasmine immediately recognized a few faces as she and Patrick approached. There was Randy Ballard, the grocery store manager. He was a quiet man, always nice enough, and he had worked at the Shoppe Right as long as she could remember.

Not far away from him was Julie Barnes, the editor of the Cove Herald and a local celebrity who was loved and hated by equal proportions of the townspeople. For some reason, the handsome and well-dressed older woman had her eyes fixed intently on Randy.

Cynthia Jackson was also there, her brow knitted in some sort of pained grimace. Luffy got excited at first, until he realized Teresa was not in residence.

As Jasmine made her way through the crowd, she suddenly felt a hand on her shoulder. She looked back and saw her father. Her mother was there beside him. She let her father pull her in close. Luffy squeezed in between all three sets of legs and hunkered down, looking around nervously at the surging crowd.

A moment later they were joined by the eternally happy Ruby Evans, their next-door neighbor and the voracious reader who often dumped huge loads of books on Patrick at the Nook. Ruby gave Jasmine one of her signature hugs, then gave Luffy a few pets. For once, she did not look very happy at all. It seemed she had been crying.

"If I can have your attention," a voice boomed from the steps of the tiny town hall building.

The crowd murmur quickly died away as everyone turned toward the speaker. It was Sheriff Lustbader, a dark, usually soft-spoken man who was one of only four full time employees at the Blackwood Cove police department. He was standing before a microphone stand. A large speaker had been set up behind him, in order to broadcast his voice across the commons.

"If I can have your full attention for the next few minutes," Lustbader continued, "we can settle as much of this matter with you as possible. After that I will take a few questions. If that sounds alright to everybody?"

He looked around uncertainly. He had never done this before. Of course plenty of people had died in the Cove, but not since his predecessor was in office had anyone died in a manner that necessitated a public address.

"Okay," Lustbader went on. "As you've all heard by now, our very own Jack Torres was found dead this morning. His body was discovered at about a quarter past eight. We took a great deal of care at the scene, as should always be the case, and we weren't able to establish a cause of death until a few hours later. Jack was found drifting in the surf about twenty feet off the beach, not far from the docks. We believe that he perished sometime between eleven PM last night and five this morning. He was last seen exiting the Leaky Trawler at half past ten, and witnesses claim he was highly intoxicated. We think this state of inebriation was a major contributing factor in his death.

"We found water in Jack's lungs. A great deal of it. He died of drowning, and we're pretty much certain about that. I know what you all might be thinking. How could Jack Torres go out like this? Men don't often die doing what they're the best at. That would be like our own mayor dying because he took too long of a nap."

There was laughter all around. In particular, Jasmine heard a throaty roar from somewhere nearby that was recognizable as the mayor himself, Eugene Carter.

"Why are they laughing?" Ruby asked. "This isn't the time for laughing."

"It's alright," Peter Moore said. "That's how a lot of people deal with bad things."

But, Jasmine thought, this specific death would not be seen as bad by most people in the Cove. It had been many years since Crazy Jack, as he was called, had been accepted by anyone but Ruby herself.

"Yes, Jack Torres was a seasoned sailor," Sheriff Lustbader went on. "He was the last person we would have expected to succumb to the water. But tragedies don't often make sense. Accidents happen. You hear about things like this all the time. An experienced race car driver might die in a horrible car crash, or something like that. Jack Torres thought highly of his skills in the water, and for good reason. But, last night, circumstances must have been such that his confidence was misplaced for the first time. That is all we can really say about the why for right now.

"As for what we will do next," Lustbader added, "we have no reason at all to believe foul play was involved in Jack's death. As of right now there is no plan to call in additional help from a larger law enforcement department. Blackwood Cove has not seen a murder in thirty-nine years, and it seems we will at least make it to forty before the next one. Now, I will be taking questions. One at a time, please. Raise your hands."

The first person called upon was Cliff Adams. "Do you know where Jack's boat is?"

"Good question," said Lustbader. "No, we don't. It isn't tied up at the docks. Jack must have taken it out in the dark last night and had some mishap. Perhaps it will run ashore somewhere in the next few days. Next question."

"Do you think Jack might have died on purpose?" someone else asked.

"As in, did he commit suicide," Lustbader translated. "No, I don't think so. Jack didn't strike me as the sort of man to internalize his pain, to put it lightly. We have all had our run-ins and altercations with him."

The next person called upon was Marsha Cargill, the Cove's resident conspiracy theorist and paranoiac. The sheriff realized his mistake immediately, but it was too late.

"Is there something going on here that we need to know about?" Marsha belted out. "Is there something you aren't telling us, sheriff?"

Lustbader smiled in confusion. "About what, Ms. Cargill?"
"About the sea!" she shrieked in reply. "Something out at sea is causing problems! Last month we had all those dead fish washing up on the beach! And now we have Jack Torres. Your very own 'Crazy Jack,' people! Something is going on here, and I intend to get to bottom of it, even if our police department insists on pulling the wool over our eyes!"

Sheriff Lustbader raised his hands in a placating gesture. His soft voice was nearly drowned out by Marsha's continued yelling, but he persisted.

"If there is something strange happening, somehow," he said, "we don't know any more about it than you do. We're Cove people just like all of you. Born and raised. I don't understand how-"

"Because they've gotten to you!" Marsha yelled, pointing an accusing finger at the sheriff. "Because the government has invaded your department. They have their hooks in every town across America, some even smaller than Blackwood Cove! Mark my words, by this time on Saturday we'll have FBI agents crawling all over the town making sure no one is asking too many questions! Except you won't *know* they're FBI. They'll pretend to be tourists, or something!"

"Alright, that's enough!" Lustbader finally barked, raising his voice for perhaps the fifth time in his entire life. "I've had it with you for tonight, Marsha. Your fellow townspeople have been through enough today without you upsetting them with your crap. Now go home, or I'll have you detained in the department overnight."

"On what grounds?" Marsha demanded, her jaw sticking out like that of a bulldog.

"For disturbing the peace," Lustbader replied. "Please leave now."

"Fine," Marsha said, turning around and beginning to push her way through the crowd. "Fine, don't listen to me. Any of you. We'll see who's right in the end. We'll see!"

Meanwhile, the sheriff shook his head and let out an exasperated sigh.

"I think that about does it for the questions tonight," he said. "If you really must know more, feel free to stop by the station in a little while."

***

As Jasmine walked along with Luffy at her side, she looked around and realized she seemed to be the only one who was taking the sheriff up on his offer. Other than the Leaky Trawler, Main Street was dead and silent. Everyone had either gone home or had retired to the bar for the evening.

The sun was already setting further inland, a great fiery orb descending into the deep green of the forest. Its blazing rays stabbed eastward through the sky, and where they hit the heavy fog and cloud cover over the Cove they seemed to multiply, like the light from a lighthouse reflecting off lenses. The sky looked like one giant, mottled peach. The mist that filled the town glowed and became white smoke, parting before Jasmine and curling back in behind her.

"Did you see Brandon?" Luffy asked.

Jasmine nodded. The young man had looked more shocked than anything. He had been at the address with his mother, Amy Watson. Amy was the sister of Jack Torres, estranged from him in just about every way possible. Jasmine didn't think the woman and her brother had so much as spoken in years, but Amy had still looked overcome by grief. Her son was there mostly as a crutch, holding her up so she didn't collapse onto the ground.

Perhaps, Jasmine thought with a frown, Amy was feeling some regrets of her own. Regrets of a familial relationship too quickly and easily discarded. When Jack was alive, the gulf between them must have seemed too large to bridge. But in the wake of death, the finality of it, all challenges must pale in comparison. Perhaps Amy thought she should have tried harder.

"Maybe you should go out with him now," Luffy suggested. "Just to take his mind off of things."

"That's the wrong reason to go out on a date with someone, Luffy," Jasmine said quietly, peering around her, trying to see through the murky mist. If she didn't already know this town like the back of her hand, she might have declared herself lost.

"How would you know?" Luffy asked. "Have you been on a date before?"

"Can it," Jasmine said firmly. "I'm thinking about a bit more than that right now. Maybe it's difficult for you to understand, but life is about more than having a good time."

"I'm a dog, Jasmine. But that doesn't make me stupid. I had a whole life before we even met, remember."

"Luffy," Jasmine said with a chuckle, "you were probably a year old when I found you. Besides, you've told me a thousand times that you don't remember anything from before we met."

"I don't," Luffy agreed. "But I'm sure I was doing something, right?"

***

The Blackwood Cove police department stood at one end of a small roadside park on Cypress Street. Jasmine detoured into the park briefly to let Luffy take care of some business. While she was standing there in the dewy grass, waiting for him to wrap things up, she saw a black SUV rolling along the street. It stopped outside the police department, and the three cops from the public address soon piled out and marched inside.

"I guess they're back," said Luffy, briefly sniffing the spot he had just watered. "Perfect timing. You don't think they'll have a problem with me coming inside, do you?"

Jasmine grinned. "We're taxpayers, Luffy. We pay their salaries. So if they do say anything, we'll just ignore them. It's not like they're cops. Not really. They're just guys from the Cove who thought it would be a fun job. Sitting around, drinking coffee and eating donuts all day."

They were good guys, too. She knew all of them, had known them since she was a little girl. And that was how she also knew that, when it came to investigating the death of Jack Torres, they were in over their heads.

So she and Luffy stepped into the police station. The sheriff was still there in the lobby, talking quietly with the woman at the reception desk. At the sound of the door he turned around, looking guarded and nervous. Perhaps he expected a stampede of concerned citizens. Or else he was afraid he might see Marsha Cargill again, sprinting in to give him a piece of her disjointed mind.

"Jasmine Moore!" Lustbader said with obvious relief. "And her pal, Luffy! I thought I saw you earlier. What can I do for you?"

"Don't get too excited," Jasmine said. "Because I might be about to come across as another Marsha Cargill."

The sheriff frowned. "Oh. Well, what is it?"

All of a sudden, Jasmine felt foolish. She felt like a tiny girl role playing as something she wasn't. The urge to leave surged up inside her, the need to escape, but she pushed it back down.

"I don't think Jack Torres drowned," she said.

Lustbader smiled. "Well, it was confirmed that drowning was

the cause of death. His lungs were full of water, which means he was still breathing, still alive, when he was submerged."

"Right," said Jasmine, feeling the burn of embarrassment. "What I *meant* to say was, I don't think it was an accident. I think he was murdered."

To her surprise, Lustbader didn't immediately laugh. Nor did he shut her down. He just nodded his head and gestured to her.

"Why don't we sit down in my office?" he said. "Do you drink coffee?"

"Sometimes," Jasmine replied.

She was led down a narrow hallway. The floor was old, faded linoleum and the walls were dark brown paneling straight out of the '80s. They stopped at a small break room, where Lustbader poured them both a cup of coffee. He asked how she liked hers, she instructed him, and a few moments later they were taking a seat in the sheriff's office.

She hadn't been expecting much, but even so the room wasn't nearly as glamorous as she thought it would be. The walls were more brown paneling. The desk was an antique, leftover from three sheriffs ago, but it was so beat up that it probably held little residual value. There was an American flag in one corner. A picture of Lustbader's wife and kids on the desk. And that was all.

"Now, what makes you think he was murdered?" the sheriff asked, taking a sip of coffee. She didn't know how he did it. The stuff was still lava hot. Maybe he had callused his lips, tongue and throat enough that it no longer bothered him, the same way her mom could do dishes with her bare hands in scalding hot water.

"It's obvious, isn't it?" Jasmine asked, hoping that would be sufficient. Because she was worried that, if she really started talking, she was just sound even more foolish than she felt.

"I suppose it would be easy to jump to the conclusion of murder without the knowledge we now have," Lustbader admitted. "We all know Jack was an excellent swimmer. He had the endurance of a Greek god. And he had so much seafaring experience he could have written a training manual for the Navy. Is that about in line with your thinking, Jasmine?"

She nodded, gripping her cup nervously.

"But don't let me speak for you," Lustbader went on, leaning back in his chair and spreading his hands. "You're a citizen of this town just like I am. Use your own words. Go on, I'm listening."

Jasmine bit her lip. "Well..."

"He said to go on," Luffy told her, nudging her hand with his cold, wet nose.

"Jack Torres once swam fifteen miles in the worst storm in Cove history," she finally said. "He had a life vest, yeah, but that's still an incredible feat. Are you telling me he drowned in calm water?"

"That's what I'm telling you," the sheriff said. "The water was calm when he was found, that's true. But it wasn't that calm all night. Remember, he could have drowned as early as eleven PM."

"But there wasn't a storm or anything!" Jasmine replied. "He took his boat out, right? It's missing from the dock, like you said. What could possibly have happened that he would end up in the water without a life vest?"

"That is a great question," Lustbader said. "One we might never have the answer to. But here's how I'm looking at it. The only reason he did die was that, by some strange occurrence, he was forced to enter the water without that life vest. The very same technology that allowed him to stay afloat in that terrible storm back in the day. He had it then, he didn't have it now. That's the difference between living and dying."

Jasmine shook her head, opening her mouth to speak. But she could think of nothing else to say.

"This has been a horrible shock for all of us," said Lustbader. "Death is almost never an easy thing to wrap your mind around. I think once you wake up tomorrow morning, after a night's rest, it will start making a lot more sense. We obviously don't have the whole story, but all the evidence we have now says Jack died of drowning. He was drunk. Witnesses at the Trawler said he had gone on one heck of a bender that night. The guy was nowhere near as fit, physically or mentally, as he was back during that storm. The mighty rise, the mighty fall, and that's the way of the world. Unfortunately. As far as the department is concerned, Ms. Moore, this case is closed."

The sheriff took a long drink of coffee and then smiled gently at her, as though the conversation was over.

"I respect your opinion, sheriff," Jasmine said. "But I don't agree with it. And I don't want Marsha Cargill to be the only person conducting an alternative investigation."

"That woman is all talk," the sheriff said. "But if you really want to investigate this, Jasmine, I can't and won't stop you. I could *advise* you to stop, but I won't do that either. As far as I'm concerned, there's no danger involved in it. I'll tell you what..."

He sat forward now, grabbing a pen and a sheet of paper.

"I'll even give you my blessing," he went on, writing out a quick note and then signing his name under it. He folded the sheet of paper up and slid it across to her. "If anyone wants to give you grief, just show them this. Heck, tell them you've been deputized for all I care."

"Thanks, sheriff," she said, hardly believing her ears.

"But I'm just curious about one thing," Lustbader said now, holding up a finger. "Correct me if I'm wrong, but you didn't know Jack Torres personally. Like the rest of the kids in town, the extent of your experience with him was probably walking past his cottage on Halloween night for a good scare. And it's no secret that Jack wasn't well liked around the Cove. So, why do you care so much about what happened to him?"

She had been thinking about that herself on the walk over. And it so happened that she had managed to puzzle it out.

"It's simple, sheriff," she said. "If you happen to be wrong, and there *is* a murderer in this town, I don't really want them running around free."

The sheriff nodded, raising his eyebrows. "Okay. Godspeed, Deputy."

"Also," Luffy added, "you're a bit of an overachiever, Jasmine."

CHAPTER 5

"Was all that true, what you said back there?" Luffy asked.

They were nearly back home, now. The fire in the sky had died, the sun had vanished, and now they could see a few faint ghosts of stars above them, through the heavy blanket of cloud that never seemed to leave. Jasmine's stomach growled with hunger. However, food was the last thing on her mind. She knew Luffy would wolf down his dinner with the usual enthusiasm, barely waiting to taste any of it before it was down his throat. But the more she thought about what she had just done, and what she was going to do next, the further her appetite seemed to retreat.

"Was what true?" she asked after a moment.

"About why you're doing this," said Luffy. "You can fool Sheriff Lustbader, Jasmine, but you can't fool me. I smelled something else on you. Either you were lying, or it wasn't the whole truth."

"I wasn't *lying*," Jasmine snapped, with more venom than she meant. "Who wants to live in a town with a murderer? Especially a *small* town, where your chance of being his next victim is higher."

"Or *her* next victim," Luffy pointed out.

"Touché." She thought about apologizing for her snippy behavior, but Luffy was a dog. Forgiveness was what dogs did. He had probably already forgotten about it.

"Anyway," she added after a long silence, as they trekked

through the evening fog that had rolled in like waves of cotton candy. "It wasn't a lie. Not at all. But it wasn't the whole truth. I didn't like Jack, obviously. I'm not broken up about what happened to him. But there's certain things that separate us from the animals... no offense."

"No offense?" Luffy asked. "Are you trying to imply I'm an animal?"

"No," she said with a smile. "You're just a furry human who walks on four legs."

"That's more like it. Now go on. Tell me about what separates us from the animals."

"Well, civilization for one thing. In the wild, if a deer or something breaks its leg, it's on its own. No one will help it. The greatest assistance will come from the next predator who it crosses paths with. A mercy killing."

"Okay, I don't follow."

"Humans take care of each other, Luffy. Some animals do too, like elephants and dogs, but not in the same way. Because they don't know how to. If a person breaks their leg, other humans will carry them or at least help them walk. They'll bring food and let the wounded person rest and heal. That's the bedrock of civilization; working together, helping each other out."

"Okay. Now I'm starting to get it. Crazy Jack didn't have a broken leg, but he did have a broken personality."

"Right. And maybe we weren't all very friendly with him, but it's not like we drove him out of town. He got his groceries at the Shoppe Right like the rest of us. He got his hair cut at the barbershop on Main Street."

"Every six months, when he remembered to," Luffy added.

"But the point is," Jasmine said, "he was part of the Cove, just like all of us. And moreover, he was a human being. No matter how much of a jerk he was, he still doesn't deserve to be pushed aside and written off now that he's dead. He deserves the same care and respect as anyone else. Call me an idealistic teenager..."

"I would never dream of it."

"...but I really believe in this. I'll bet I'm not the only one in town who's having doubts about how Jack died. Far from it. But I don't think anyone else cares. Not even Marsha Cargill. She's just using his death as an opportunity to stir up trouble. And if no one else is going to give Jack a fair shot at justice, on the off chance he *was* murdered, then I guess I'll have to do it. And I have the time."

"You work at the Nook three days a week," Luffy reminded her.

"Yes, and I usually have three or four training appointments every week too," Jasmine replied. "I'm not planning on interrupting my schedule. But in between shifts and appointments, I'm going to be the best investigator I can be. And you're going to help me."

Luffy's ears went back and he made a whining sound. "Help?"

"Yes! You're an honorary human, right? And humans help each other."

"But... I've never investigated before."

She smiled, ruffling the fur on his head. "Sure you have. Every time you go smelling around a fire hydrant or sniffing another dog's butt. That's investigating."

"If you say so," Luffy said uncertainly.

"Anyway, we're deputies now. This piece of paper is going to give us all the power we need."

They were passing under a street lamp, glowing yellowish orange in the gathering darkness. Jasmine paused and took the note Lustbader had given her out of her pocket. She unfolded it and read it for the first time.

By signing this note, I, Sheriff Kenneth Lustbader, give my blessings and my support to Jasmine Moore. Her questions, inquiries and explorations should be viewed as a community service, and should not be hampered in any case other than if the investigator finds herself accidentally in breach of the law.

Just below, in big swirling letters, was his signature. Jasmine felt giddy as she looked down at it. She knew what it was. What Lustbader *thought* it was, anyway. He thought he was just setting a child's mind at ease, giving her something to do so her boredom and restlessness wouldn't cause him greater trouble.

To use Barry Brock's words, he had thrown a quarter to the kid's lemonade stand.

But Jasmine was going to prove them all wrong.

"Who were you talking to?" a voice suddenly asked.

Fear shot up Jasmine's spine like a bolt of electricity. She quickly stuffed the note back into her pocket and turned around. Brandon Watson was crossing the street toward her, smiling, his cheeks as ruddy as usual but his eyes clear. It seemed he had gotten some rest.

"No one!" Jasmine said with a smile, feeling her own cheeks going red. "Just myself."

For some reason, almost as if he didn't recognize the young man, Luffy flattened his ears and let out a deep growl.

Brandon stopped short, looking down at the dog in shock. After a moment, he let out nervous laughter. "Easy boy! It's just me. What's gotten into him, anyway?"

"No idea," Jasmine asked, just as shocked as he was. "It's OK, Luffy. Relax."

The dog sat, and soon was back to his normal happy self, panting away in the cool, damp air.

"Oh!" Jasmine said, suddenly remembering something. "I'm really sorry about your uncle, Brandon. I can't imagine-"

"It's OK," Brandon broke in. "You don't have to say all that stuff to me, Jaz. To be honest, I'm not really sad about it. I'm just kind of in shock, or something. I feel like everything's in limbo. I've just been walking around ever since I got my mom home. I just feel kind of weird, you know?"

Jasmine nodded. "I know exactly what you mean. I've felt that way before too."

Brandon smiled, stepping closer. "But I feel a lot better now that... we're talking."

That was about as close to flirting as the nervous kid got. Luckily for him, Jasmine knew him better than he knew himself.

"If you need anything," she said, "let me know. And I don't mean that in the fake, bullcrap way. Like, I really mean it. Okay?"

Brandon nodded. "Sure. Okay. Cool. Actually, maybe I *would* feel better if..."

"If what?" Jasmine asked.

"Nah, never mind," Brandon quickly replied. "I guess I'll see you tomorrow, Jaz. You too, Luffy. Hopefully you don't bite my arm off next time I see you."

He waved and then took off again, crossing the road and continuing his walk. It didn't seem he was heading back home just yet. He had some more walking to do. Trying to clear his mind. Which could be hard in the Cove, with the weight of the past pressing in around you.

"What was that all about, anyway?" Jasmine asked. "You never growl at Brandon. You've known him as long as you've known me!"

"I dunno," Luffy replied. "I just got a bad feeling, out of nowhere. Maybe it has something to do with this morning."

"What about it?"

"Well, I'll spell it out for you, inspector. The very morning after his uncle died, which you, by the way, suspect to be murder, Brandon shows up acting all squirrely. Squirrels! I love squirrels. I love to chase them..."

"Get back on track," Jasmine said.

"Right. Well, don't you think it was kinda weird? He was obviously doing something all night, and it wasn't sleeping. And then he asks you to take his shift. He's never done that before. And why? Because he had 'things to do' or whatever it was he said."

"He could have been taking care of evidence," Jasmine said, her mouth falling open.

"Exactly!"

"Or he might have been gaming all night. It wouldn't have been the first time."

"Well, if that was all it was, he would have said that."

Jasmine nodded. Luffy was right. Brandon was hiding something. She didn't think it was murder... but, much to her despair, she couldn't rule it out. Not yet.

**

Her alarm went off at seven AM, the usual time. Jasmine was up and out of bed in two seconds flat, excitement and fear coursing through her veins in equal measure as she remembered her investigation.

She hit the alarm to turn it off. And then she fell straight to the floor, crumpling into a heap. Luffy ran over, licking at her face and then nestling in close, whining as his eyes shifted left and right nervously. In a moment Jasmine suddenly gasped for air and sat up, looking around wildly.

She was shaking from top to bottom as she crawled over to her desk and pulled out her notes to make a fourth entry.

4 - *Cynthia Jackson is in the bookstore. She and Patrick are arguing about something.*

"Hello?" Luffy said. "I can't read. What was it?"

Jasmine told him.

"Is that it?" he asked.

"Yeah, that was it. And thanks, I'm doing OK."

Luffy's tail waggled shamefully. "They're happening more often, Jasmine."

"I figured that out."

"What are we going to do? Go to a doctor?"

"No!" said Jasmine. "There's nothing wrong with me."

"Maybe we should tell your parents."

She gave him a withering look that said everything. Luffy marched over to her, giving her a lick on the face.

"Maybe you should take it easy today," he suggested.

She shook her head. "I'm fine now. I feel like I just woke up from a nightmare, is all. Besides, we need to start our investigation."

***

The door opened only a few seconds after Jasmine rang the bell. Ruby Evans stood there inside, wearing a smile and about half of her usual makeup. It seemed she was partway into getting ready for the day. She wasn't even fully dressed yet, still in the tank top and shorts she had gone to bed in.

"Jaz!" she said, flinging out her arms and bundling the

younger woman into a big, warm hug. "I'm glad you've come over! I really needed to see a friendly face today."

Jasmine smiled. "Sorry, Ruby. I didn't know you were working today."

"Oh, not until ten," Ruby replied, waving a hand. "I've been lying awake since five AM, and I finally decided enough was enough. I thought I might as well just get up and ready, that way I could relax for a little bit before I had to leave."

"That's a relief," Jasmine said, "because I wondered if we could talk for a little bit. It shouldn't take longer than fifteen minutes."

"You had to ask?" Ruby replied with a grin, shepherding Jasmine inside and shutting the door. "Since when did we start rationing out our friendship in quarter hour segments?"

"Since never. This is something different, Ruby. I'm not here for just a casual chat."

"Oh. Well then, what is it? Did you have breakfast?"

Jasmine hadn't, but she nodded anyway and followed Ruby into the kitchen. Ruby poured them both a fresh cup of coffee and they sat. Meanwhile, Luffy went to stare out the sliding glass window at the birds and squirrels in the backyard.

"It's about Jack," Jasmine said after a moment, letting out a sigh.

"Oh," Ruby said again, her demeanor changing from bubbly to rather morose.

"We don't have to, though," Jasmine said quickly.

"No, that's alright," Ruby said, taking a sip of coffee as her eyes stared into space. "I think it's good to talk about these things. Otherwise you just never get them out of your head. They fester."

Jasmine winced. "Actually... I had a more practical conversation in mind."

By way of explanation, so that she wouldn't have to find the words, she pulled out Lustbader's note and slid it over. Ruby unfolded it slowly and let her eyes wander over it.

"I see," she said, her voice unreadable. "So you also think Jack was..."

"Murdered," Jasmine finished for her.

Ruby abruptly folded the note over again and slid it back. "I don't know if I have the same opinion, Jasmine. But if you have any questions, I'll be sure to answer them to the best of my ability. Because we're friends."

Jasmine's heart thumped. Shame, guilt and fear pulsed through her all at once. Was she doing the wrong thing? Should she have waited a week, and let everyone settle down?

But she had her questions. She was already here, and if she waited a week Ruby might not agree to speak with her. By then, the memory of Jack Torres would already have been paved over. The town would have moved on. No one would care enough to entertain her "investigation." She knew the Cove, she knew its people, and she knew it had to be now.

"In your own words," Jasmine said, trying to switch over into professional mode, "describe your relationship with Jack Torres."

Ruby finally smiled, perhaps entertained by her young friend's attempt at playing detective. "Aren't you going to take notes?"

Jasmine nodded, pulling out her phone. "I can record this conversation as a voice memo. If you don't mind."

"Go ahead."

Jasmine hit record and set the phone in the middle of the table. She took a long sip of coffee, watching Ruby, waiting for her to do or say something at all.

Ruby's demeanor had changed yet again. She now looked on the verge of giddiness.

"I feel like I'm in a detective story," she said.

"This lady reads too many books," Luffy called across the room.

Jasmine suppressed a smile. "Go on, Ruby. In your own words."

Her neighbor nodded. "Ok. Yes. Let's see... I wouldn't really say Jack and I had much of a relationship. I tried to treat him like a neighbor, even though my efforts were never reciprocated. I once asked Jack if he would like to visit my home for Christmas dinner. He looked at me like I had just asked him to stand on one hand and clap out the tune of 'Jingle Bells' with his feet."

"When was this?" Jasmine asked.

"About three years ago. No... four."

"You always visited Jack around the holidays, right?"

Ruby nodded. "Every year. Thanksgiving and Christmas. I was the only one, even among his family, to extend any sort of cheer his way. I would bring him a plate of food and wish him Happy Holidays. Like I said, he never much cared for my efforts. But I'm sure he at least ate the turkey and the mashed potatoes." She paused to let out a sigh. "I guess right about now I'm wondering why I ever bothered. If the man wanted anything to do with that sort of thing, with being part of the community, I think he would have at least given me a 'thank you.' But he never did. Not once."

"That didn't stop you from trying."

"No." Ruby smiled to herself, picking at a bit of peeling laminate at the edge of the table. "When I was seven years old... but, well that's ancient history. You don't want to hear about that."

"I do, actually," said Jasmine. "I want to hear whatever you feel like telling me, Ruby."

"Well, don't say I didn't warn you. When I was seven... and the Cove was very different back then. It was still up and coming, in a way. It hadn't yet seen the height of its glory, but it was busier than it is today. There were far more children, too. I was in grade school, and Jack was one year above me.... One day, at recess, I decided to get adventurous. The play area we had could no longer contain me and my wild ideas. I needed something more. So I had the bright idea of climbing over the chain link fence at the edge of the yard.

"Well, I made it over just fine. Off I went into the forest... it's the parking lot of that closed down liquor store these days. It's all crumbling asphalt now, but back then it was wilderness, teeming with life. Looking back, it was probably less than half an acre of woodland between the school and the next road over, but as a child it felt like an endless paradise. I ran wild until I heard the bell ring, and then I returned to the fence. This time, however, my climb over it did not go as planned. Unbeknownst to me, the hem of my dress had gotten caught on a jutting piece of wire so that when I tried hopping down on the other side, I found myself hanging there a few inches off the ground. Swinging back and forth, my modesty spoiled.

"But that wasn't the worst of it. The worst was how the other children reacted. All of them, boys and girls together, quickly gathered around. They pointed and laughed at me. I was a great source of amusement to them. The shy bookworm who never spoke a word in class unless she absolutely had to. Hanging there on the fence with her pretty little dress ripped and ruined. I almost died of embarrassment. And *anger*. I was so angry, Jaz. Not just at the kids but at the fence, at the dress, at my mom for buying it for me, at the entire universe and even fate itself for leading me to that moment.

"But then, I looked to one side and I saw one kid who wasn't laughing or pointing. It was Jack Torres, and he was frowning. After a long moment he finally stepped forward and helped me down. I will never forget that moment... the way he wrapped one arm around me and lifted, using his other hand to un-snag my dress. He even walked with me back into the school. I'm sure his presence that day was the only reason I wasn't teased mercilessly for the rest of the school year."

Ruby's story came to a close, and she took a deep breath and then an even deeper swallow of coffee. By the time she set the cup down, her eyes were damp with tears.

"Now you know, Jaz," she added. "Because of what happened that day, I believed that Jack Torres possessed more humanity than any one of my peers. But as my peers grew older, matured and became friendlier to me, Jack retreated into himself. The roles were reversed, and I never again saw his warm side. But in middle school, as Jack was starting to withdraw, I vowed to never give up on him. And that was a promise I kept. Until..."

Until he died. Jasmine assumed that was what the woman

was going to say. She didn't press further on that point. To do so would be unnecessarily cruel.

"Ruby, if you don't mind me asking," Jasmine said, "who else was in the schoolyard that day? Besides you and Jack?"

"Oh, that doesn't matter," Ruby replied, grabbing a tissue from a box on the nearby counter. "They're all lovely people these days."

"Humor my youthful curiosity," Jasmine suggested with a smile.

"Well, it's hard to remember specifically," Ruby replied, her eyes going distant again. "For one, our very own Mayor Eugene Carter was there. And I think so was Julie Barnes. But you mustn't think they're cruel, Jasmine. When someone fails climbing over a fence, you don't stop to think about their feelings. Not when you're a child. You just laugh, because something funny has just occurred."

"Even while she was crying and hiding her face in embarrassment?" Luffy asked, sounding doubtful.

"Thanks, Ruby," Jasmine said. "And thanks for the coffee too. It's just the way I like it. Is there anything else you can tell me? Anything strange you may have noticed about Jack or anyone else lately?"

Ruby began to shake her head, but then inspiration came to her eyes.

"There was one thing, maybe," she said. "It's probably a stretch, but the last time I was at Jack's cottage I noticed something. This was two years ago, mind, so it probably has nothing to do with anything…"

"What was it?" Jasmine asked, gripping her mug tight. "What did you see?"

"I had the impression Jack was trying to hide something under a coat he had laid out on his sofa. But I caught a glimpse under one of the edges. It looked like money. Cash. Perhaps a good amount of it. I thought that was rather odd… I didn't think Jack had ever been a very wealthy man."

"No," Jasmine agreed. "I don't think he was. He mostly lived off his severance from the old cannery, right?"

"And whatever he managed to get from selling his fishing hauls," said Ruby. She leaned forward, lowering her voice. "But I don't think he was doing much fishing the past few years. Maybe not for a long time."

"What do you mean? Are the fish not biting anymore?"

"It's not that. I just think his heart hasn't been in it. Whatever he's doing out at sea, it doesn't involve throwing nets into the water. I think he's just been looking for some alone time. Jack never fit in very well around people."

***

"No, he sure didn't," Jasmine said quietly to herself, a belated reply to the last statement of the interview.

Luffy looked up at her curiously. "So, did you get what you were after from Ruby?"

At first Jasmine nodded. But then she shrugged. She felt uncertain.

"I don't know," she said. "I feel like we're missing something. There was some question I should have asked that just never occurred to me..."

"Before you go beating yourself up," said Luffy, "let me remind you that this was your very first interview."

"I know, but..."

"But what? Did you think you could solve the murder of Jack Torres in a single morning? If it even is murder, which is only a possibility. You don't have superpowers. So, where do we go next?"

Jasmine had been trying to figure that out. She really had no logical place to go from here, so she reverted to the basic idea she had come up with last night. She had started at Ruby's house because it was the closest. Going off that, the next closest residence was that of Brandon Watson.

CHAPTER 6

"Yeah, of course I'd like to go for a walk," Brandon said. "But don't think I'm about to give your shift back to you. We traded fair and square."

He shuffled his way out through the front door of his small brick house. Over his shoulder, in the cool, dark interior, Jasmine saw the silhouette of his mother sitting rapt and numb-looking in front of the TV.

Brandon nearly tripped down the stairs as he came to meet her, owing to his haste. His feet weren't even inside his shoes all the way. He supported himself on the railing as he fixed the problem and then hopped down to the front walk. Now that he was close enough, Jasmine noticed how greasy his hair was. And his eyes were red again. He stared at her with a crazy glint in his eye, deep in the throes of exhaustion induced mania.

"Are you alright, Brandon?" she asked, reaching out to touch his arm.

He smiled. And he must have been feeling bold, because he laid one of his hands over hers.

"Yeah, I guess," he said. "I was just up late last night. Again."

"Playing games?" Jasmine asked.

Brandon shrugged. "What else?"

"What else, indeed," said Luffy. If he had been a human, he would have narrowed his eyes at that moment.

"Well," said Brandon, "where do you want to go?"

"Anywhere, really," said Jasmine. "How about the commons?"

Luffy immediately began to wag his tail.

They set off, taking their time as they wound their way through the narrow, sleepy streets of Blackwood Cove. They took a roundabout path to reach the Commons, basking in the rare autumn sunshine. It wasn't all that warm, but there was enough wind that the streets had been entirely cleared of fog. Seagulls cried in the distance, and there was the ever present but hushed sound of the ocean surf.

"I don't know what to do," Brandon suddenly said of his volition, breaking a long silence as Jasmine struggled to figure out how to begin.

"About what?" Jasmine asked.

"About my mom. She's acting like her whole world just ended. She hasn't even talked to Uncle Jack in, like, five years, so I don't know what the problem is."

"What about you? Are you still doing OK?"

"Me? Psh, yeah. I'm fine, Jaz. I barely knew the guy. I don't care that he died."

That struck Jasmine as a strange thing to say, but she chalked it up to his youthful defensiveness. He was at risk of being vulnerable, of showing some sort of emotion in front of the girl he liked, in a world that said such displays of emotion were signs of weakness.

She had to play this carefully. If her questions were too vague, she wouldn't get any answers. If they were too direct, then Brandon would shut down. He would go fully on the defensive, and act hurt. She could end up losing a good friend, all because of vague suspicion.

"What were you doing the other night?" Jasmine asked, trying to sound casual. Just a friend shooting the breeze.

"Which night?" Brandon asked, kicking at some dirt on the sidewalk and scuffing his shoe.

"Before they found Jack. I asked you that morning, but you never told me."

He glanced sidelong at her as he shoved his hands in his pockets. "Didn't I?"

"No. I asked if you were chatting to girls and you said no. But I feel like maybe you were."

"No way!" he said. "Why would I be talking to other girls? That's stupid."

And that was the reaction Jasmine was after.

"Well, you seemed kind of nervous," she said. "I'm not sure if I believe you."

"I wasn't doing anything! I was just playing games, alright? The same thing I always do."

"Then why didn't you just say that?" she asked. "I know you like to play video games. And I know you stay up all night sometimes. I have to hear Patrick complaining about it. 'That kid fell asleep on the job again!' It's not like it's a secret."

"Did he really say that to you?" Brandon asked.

"Don't change the subject," said Jasmine.

For emphasis, Luffy let out a bark.

"*What* subject?" asked Brandon. "If you don't want to believe I was playing games, then fine. If you would rather believe I was talking to some mystery girl online, go right ahead. You're the one I asked out on a date, not anyone else."

He was closing off now. Withdrawing. Once again, Jasmine felt stumped and stupid. There was some perfect chain of questions, some ideal line of questioning that a real investigator would have been able to follow. But she just couldn't seem to find it. Maybe she just wasn't being direct enough, which was something she vowed to work on. But not with Brandon. Not right now.

But maybe later.

"Okay," she said, feeling a surge of inspiration. "I still don't believe you, Brandon. But how about this. The Spyglass Diner at six o'clock tonight. A booth by the window, you and me. And you had better come armed and ready to tell me the truth, or I'm out of there before dessert. Got it?"

He looked like a man who had been drowning, and now saw a lifeline in the water. Like Jack Torres might have looked if, on that terrible stormy day when he almost died, someone from above had reached down from the sky and lifted him back onto land.

Except now Jack was dead. His triumph had turned into his tragedy. She just hoped that Brandon wouldn't follow the same course. But in the end, the truth was what really mattered.

**

The shame of what she had just done caught up to her an hour later, as she and Luffy were meandering around the commons together.

"I can't believe myself," she said, squeezing her head with both hands. "I just played Brandon like a fiddle."

"Isn't that what detectives do?" Luffy asked.

"I guess so, but..."

"No buts. Get used to it. You wanted to go after the truth, and this is what it takes. Besides, Brandon is in love with you. He's blind with it. Just don't say anything about this deputy thing, and he won't be any the wiser."

Jasmine shook her head. "No. I have to tell him. It isn't right."

"No, I'll tell you what isn't right. It isn't right to finally go out with a guy who's been crushing on you since you were three years outside diapers, and then telling him it was all so you could get your scoop. You'll break his heart."

"I'll tell him it's a dual-purpose date," Jasmine said, chewing on her lip.

Luffy eyed her. "Please. Even I know how flimsy that sounds, and I'm a dog."

"I know, I know... but it's better he hears about it now rather than later. Besides, it's not like I don't like Brandon."

"And it's not like you *do* like him. I've heard it all before, Jasmine. Save your breath for the next interview. Especially since you forgot to brush your teeth this morning. You stink!"

**

Jasmine wasn't thinking like a detective as she walked into the Shoppe Right grocery store. She had a single objective in mind, and it had nothing to do with Jack.

Situated on the very edge of town, near the main road, the

Shoppe Right was the Cove's only name in the grocery game. It wasn't nearly as large as the grocery store in the next town. But, with its six main aisles of products and its produce section, it was all the town needed.

Jasmine was in the candy aisle looking for breath mints when someone's shoes squeaked on the floor behind her. She looked back and saw Randy Ballard, the store manager, strolling along with a clipboard in his hands. He kept glancing left and right, making notes of something with a pen.

"Excuse me," Jasmine said.

He looked over, stared for a moment, and then smiled. "Oh! Hi, Jezebel."

"Jasmine," she said.

"Oh! Right. Jasmine Moore. Sorry about that. I'm a textbook example of what happens to a person's brain when they fill it up with SKU numbers. Is there something I can help you with?"

"Breath mints," she said.

Randy pointed out toward one corner of the store. "If you want the good stuff, it'll be in the pharmacy area. Right beside the antacids."

Jasmine thanked him and began walking away, but Luffy nipped at her sleeve with his teeth.

"Got it!" she whispered.

Randy Ballard had been at the address on Jack's death as well. And, Jasmine remembered, the editor of the local newspaper had been paying particular attention to him. There had to be a reason for it.

"Actually," she said, turning back around. "There's something else I would like to ask you, Mr. Ballard."

He smiled up at her again from his clipboard. He also resembled a drowning man waiting for a life line. More specifically, any chance at all to take a quick break from whatever monotonous chore he was in the middle of.

"You were at the address, right?" Jasmine asked. "About Crazy Jack?"

"I think half the town was there," he said, reaching to his right to rearrange a few scattered boxes of candy.

"Well, you were one of the people I recognized. Did you know Jack very well?"

"Not any better than most around here. But I... um..."

Randy looked around the store. He even looked behind him. When he spoke again, it was almost a whisper.

"I'm the one who found Jack that morning," he said. "In the water."

"Oh," Jasmine said, her heart thumping as she tried to figure out what this could mean.

Randy nodded. "'Oh' is right. Nasty business. You don't expect to see a dead body on your morning stroll. I guess it had to be me, though," he added, rolling his eyes.

"What do you mean?" Jasmine asked.

"Sorry," Randy said, "but this isn't the kind of thing I want to be talking about at my place of business, if you catch my drift."

Jasmine nodded, waiting for him to continue, but he didn't. He was back to counting, glancing both ways in the aisle. It seemed he was happy to end the conversation there.

Jasmine pulled out Lustbader's note and held it out.

"Mr. Ballard," she said, "I'm just trying to gather all the information I can. It would be a big help if you would tell me what you know."

He read the note, sighed, and nodded his head.

"Okay. After my shift, how about that? I'm out of here at five today, thank goodness. It's a short shift for me."

"Great!" Jasmine said. "I'll be here at five."

"No, not here," said Randy. "My place. 3301 Ivy Road. Meet me there at 6:15. Just so you know, I'm not going to feed you or anything. We'll talk for a bit, and then you're on your own."

"That's fine," she replied with a smile. "I've already made dinner arrangements."

**

Feeling out of sorts and sucking on a breath mint, Jasmine found herself wandering back home. She had barely made it to her bed when another vision struck, causing her limp body to collapse onto the mattress. She came back to reality a moment later with Luffy licking her cheek.

"This is getting out of hand," he said.

She sat up, blinking a few times to bring the world back into focus. "I know. But at least I know what they feel like, now. I can see them coming. This isn't going to stop me."

"Maybe it should," Luffy suggested. "I'd be the first one to tell you that not everything in this town is as it should be, but that's a far cry from murder. You do know that Jack Torres probably did just drown, right?"

"I know. But I'm not convinced. And neither are you."

"Fair enough."

This time, she read the entry aloud as she scrawled it in her notes, so that Luffy could hear it.

5 - A black man in a raincoat is standing on the beach. He doesn't seem to care that he's being soaked not only by the rain but by the waves that keep washing over his shoes.

"Was it Donald Parks?" Luffy asked, referring to one of the few African American people who lived in the Cove. He was also somewhat of a hermit, and lived near the beach on his own, not far from Jack's cottage. But unlike the dead man, Donald was well liked in the town, if a bit shy.

"No," Jasmine replied. "The guy I just saw was a lot younger. In his late twenties or early thirties. I've never seen him before."

"Probably because he isn't real," said Luffy. "I'm starting to think they're just dreams, Jasmine. You need to see a doctor."

She stood up from her desk, feeling much better. By then it was close to lunch time, and the lack of a breakfast had caught up to her. Not to mention the coffee she had drank at Ruby's house, making her empty stomach feel sour.

Her father was at work, and her mother had gone out shopping. Jasmine quickly put together a sandwich and carried it up to her room. For the next several hours, she plotted out the course of her investigation, wrote up lists of questions, and even printed out a map of the Cove that she could make notes on.

By the time she left the house again to meet Randy Ballard,

her room was starting to look like it belonged to some crazy conspiracy theorist. The only thing missing was the red yarn crisscrossing the wall. It was exactly what she had envisioned, and now she had a firm grasp of what she was doing.

***

Randy Ballard lived alone in a house that was far too large for him. He and his wife had divorced several years ago, and she now lived a few cities away near her family. The couple had children, but they were currently away at college. As Jasmine stepped inside the place, the immediate impression she had was of an empty shell. A hollow place full of echoing memories.

Randy shut the door behind her and turned to regard her, looking rather less nervous than he had earlier. He had already showered and changed into his evening attire; plaid pajama bottoms, a knitted sweater, and a pair of slippers that looked to be a decade old at least.

"Can I get you anything to drink, officer?" Randy asked with a smile.

"No, I'm fine," she said. "I don't want to take up too much of your time, Mr. Ballard. Why don't we sit down and get started?"

He nodded, gesturing for Jasmine to continue down the hall. They were soon seated in his living room, him on a couch that looked to be on the verge of collapse, and Jasmine on an armchair that looked like it had spent half of its life outside. It was lumpy and uncomfortable. There was barely any cushioning left in it. And the floor below, once beautifully polished hardwood, was covered in dust and grime. It seemed, in the absence of his family, Randy had lost any and all enthusiasm for housekeeping.

"Sorry about the mess," he said belatedly. "I don't spend much time at home these days."

"What do you do after work, then?" she asked.

He shrugged. "I usually eat out. I go for long walks, and visit a few friends along the way. I don't really like to be here until I'm ready to go to bed. Too many memories. I keep meaning to sell the place, but..."

Jasmine nodded. "You don't have to explain the state of your residence to me, Mr. Ballard. But I would like you to clarify the remarks you made at the store earlier. And expand upon them."

"Of course." Randy glanced at Luffy, who was sitting by his owner's side obediently. "That's why the two of you came. To sniff out my secrets, right?"

"Oh, there's plenty to sniff in this house," Luffy remarked. "I think he had pizza last night. Maybe there's a few pieces of crust left in the garbage. Maybe I should-"

Jasmine laid a hand on his neck, keeping him there.

"Like I said before," Randy went on. "I didn't know Jack Torres any better than the next guy. But he seemed to think he knew me very well."

"Oh?" said Jasmine, slyly pulling out her phone, hitting record, and leaving it face down on the arm of the chair.

"The guy was really crazy!" Randy said with a grin. "You should have heard the crap he was trying to spread about me. I guess you *would* have heard it, if everyone in town didn't automatically believe he was lying. The rumors didn't exactly catch fire, if you know what I mean."

"What did he say?"

"That I was a crook! Can you believe it? And I don't mean a crook the way that Cargill lady seems to think. She believes I charge one cent more per item than every other store in the state, and I pocket all those extra pennies, and it's a racket that the whole government knows about including the CIA and they're in on it, blah blah, yadda, yadda."

"That sounds like something she'd say," Jasmine said. "But what about Jack?"

"His story was a little more detailed and realistic. According to him, my grocery store was just a front. I don't know what exactly he thought I was doing... laundering money for drug kingpins or something... but he actually seemed downright convinced. He even claimed to have proof, but of course it never materialized. That didn't stop him from harassing me continuously, however."

"I guess they didn't call him Crazy Jack for nothing," said

Luffy.

But was it crazy? Or had Jack stumbled on to something? Had he been silenced? Jasmine narrowed her eyes, staring at Randy. He was a nice man. She had known him all her life, and nothing he ever did or said had ever struck her as being odd. But at that moment, sitting in this filthy house with a man over twice her age, Jasmine suddenly started to feel very claustrophobic.

However, Randy seemed unperturbed. He sat calmly on the sofa, waiting for the next question.

Jasmine cleared her throat. "When was the last time you saw Jack Torres alive?"

Randy nodded. "That's easy. It was at the Trawler that night. The night before I found him in the water."

Jasmine and Luffy shared a look.

"Did you see or hear anything strange that night?" Jasmine asked.

"No stranger than usual. I was none too sober myself, but Jack was absolutely blasted. He could barely walk, but he still found it in him to visit my seat at the bar and start on one of his tirades. It was a good thing his speech was so slurred that no one else could hear him, because he said some pretty nasty things. How he was going to put a stop to what I was doing. How he was going to show everyone in the Cove who he was. And he kept saying something about Cynthia Jackson and Patrick, your boss at The Book Nook."

"What about them?" Jasmine asked, her heart thumping.

"Something about how they were conspiring against him in some way, and it had been going on for years." Randy shrugged. "Like I said, he was sloshed and mumbling his words. It was hard to tell what he was going on about."

"What happened after that?"

"I told him to leave me alone. I told him I had spent good money on my buzz and if he ruined it he was going to have to reimburse me. It was just a joke, but he took it seriously. He tried to hit me."

Jasmine must have looked worried, because Randy

immediately chuckled and made a placating gesture with his hands.

"Don't worry," he said. "You know those dreams where you try to do something but it feels like you're moving in slow motion and you have the strength of a newborn sloth? It was like that. I dodged the hit as easily as you'd step out of the way of an old lady on the sidewalk. Jack fell over, and that was when a few other guys decided enough was enough and escorted him out of the bar."

"Did you see where he went after that?" Jasmine asked.

"Nope. I was still in my seat, shrugging off the latest abuse from Crazy Jack. I guess he probably went towards home, but then decided a late-night cruise was the best salve for his wounded pride, and hopped on his boat. The rest is history. The guy was so drunk he probably could have drowned in a puddle."

Jasmine had been feeling doubts about her murder theory earlier today. But she had reinforced her beliefs. In her mind, someone had probably wanted Jack dead for a long time, and they had finally found the perfect moment in which to pull it off and make it seem like a big accident. It was just as good a theory, she thought, as the theory that Jack had drunkenly fallen overboard and drowned.

"Is there anything else you can tell me about Jack's recent behavior?" Jasmine asked. "Anything at all? I don't care how silly it might seem."

"You don't, do you?" Randy asked with a smile, rubbing his chin. "Well, here's a funny thing I noticed about Jack. This isn't recent though. In fact, it's years out of date. But Jack used to have a dog, too."

"Okay," Jasmine said. "But what does that have to do with anything?"

"Just hear me out. So, Jack used to buy dog food with his normal groceries every week. He did that for a while. I don't know, a year or so. But suddenly he stopped. Weeks went by; no dog food. When I asked him about it, he got this nasty, evil smile on his face and he said something I'll never forget."

"What?" Jasmine asked.

"He looked straight into my eyes, and he said, 'I hated that dog. I did what I should have done a long time ago.'" Randy sat back, staring at Jasmine with a satisfied expression on his face. "The guy killed his dog. I'm one hundred percent sure of it. Class act, huh? I wonder what Luffy would think of that."

"Oh, I'm thinking about it," Luffy said. "Now I hate Crazy Jack even more."

"The poor dog's bones are probably buried in the sand out there by his cottage," Randy went on. "I wouldn't be surprised. Heck, he might have other things buried too. You never know. I never would have wished death on the guy, but..." He threw off a lazy salute. "See ya later, Jack."

Jasmine felt shaken. She started losing the thread of questions she had planned out.

"Is there anything else?" she asked. "More recent things? Anyone Jack talked to, or said anything about?"

Randy shook his head. "Nope. I never made it a habit to pay much attention to what Jack was doing. He butted into my life often enough that I never felt the need to seek out his company outside of our little encounters. You know what I think?"

"What?" Jasmine asked.

"I think he held a grudge against me ever since I asked about his dog. That's how sensitive and quick to anger that man was. He hated me ever since that moment, and he dedicated himself to trying to mess up my life. Well, look at me now. Divorced. A woman I still love, who decided she doesn't want to see me anymore. Kids that I'll probably only get to see on holidays. But Jack's dead, and I'm still breathing. I guess I won."

He smirked then, nodding his head.

"Yes," he added after a moment. "I would say that I won."

***

Randy's last words echoed through Jasmine's mind during her walk to Main Street. She arrived at the Spyglass Diner on autopilot and didn't even realize where she was until the hostess greeted her.

"Did Brandon Watson arrive yet?" she asked.

The hostess narrowed her eyes, glancing around the small restaurant. "Um..."

"About this tall," Jasmine said, holding up a hand. "Dirty blond hair, red cheeks?"

"Oh! Yes, he's at a booth in the back. By the windows. You can go right on in."

Jasmine thanked the woman and headed inside, holding Luffy by the collar. She trusted him in almost any situation, but she knew the draw of food scraps on the floor, dropped by clumsy diners, would be too much temptation for him to bear.

Brandon was just where the hostess had said, sitting alone at a booth and staring out through the window. A fresh bank of fog had rolled in, its gray tendrils curling over the curb outside like the fingers of some vengeful ghost.

When Jasmine sat down, Brandon jumped in startlement.

"Sorry!" said Jasmine. "I thought you heard me coming."

"I did," he replied with a smile. "But... I dunno. Never mind. I was going to say something and then I realized it would sound lame."

"I appreciate your honesty. But I would like it if you just spoke your mind. Tell me what you were going to say."

He licked his lips, then stalled further by taking a long drink of his ice water. By the time he was finished with that, the waitress had arrived to ask Jasmine what she would like to drink.

"Coffee," she said immediately. Then, realizing she had already drank more coffee in the past day than she did in a typical month, she amended her request. "Decaf, please."

The waitress nodded and moved away.

"So, what was it?" Jasmine asked.

"I was going to say..." Brandon reached up to scratch his face. "That I heard you coming, but I didn't think it was you. I kind of forgot that we were actually going out on a date! Well, I didn't *forget* really, but I kind of couldn't believe it."

"You hear that?" Luffy asked. "He thinks it's a date. If you care about this kid, go along with it. You can ask your questions some other time."

"Well, do you believe it now?" Jasmine asked. "I'm sitting here. In the flesh."

"I guess so," Brandon said. "Sort of. I know you're here, but it's like I'm dreaming."

Jasmine's coffee arrived, and she proceeded to dump far too many sugar packets into it while Brandon was giving his order to the waitress. Then it was Jasmine's turn.

"Cheeseburger and fries," she said. "Extra onion, no pickles."

It was at that point that Jasmine temporarily forgot why she had come here. She and Brandon got to talking, and then they got to eating, and then back to talking again. The topic of conversation ranged from video games to school, and their plans for the future. The closest they came to talking about Jack Torres was his cat. The mean old tabby that often gave the neighborhood dogs so much grief. It seemed the ancient feline had temporarily moved in with Brandon and his mother, and had been hiding behind the sofa ever since arriving, hissing and growling occasionally.

Finally, the waitress returned and began clearing their empty plates away.

"Any dessert today?" she asked.

Brandon froze with his water cup halfway to his mouth.

"I don't know," Jasmine said, smiling. "It's up to him."

He nodded, and ordered brownies and ice cream for the both of them. It seemed like the last thing he wanted to do, and his appetite had probably died entirely, but she knew he wouldn't be able to resist a chance at extending their date.

"Happy now?" he asked as the waitress walked away to give their order to the kitchen.

"Well, not quite," Jasmine said. "You haven't fulfilled your end of the deal yet."

Brandon frowned. He looked truly unhappy. And, perhaps, somewhat afraid. Jasmine felt immediate guilt, and she very nearly called off the entire plan. There was nothing wrong with just sitting down and eating a delicious dessert with her best friend. Well, her *only* friend, really, at least of her own age.

But this was about more than friends. She had a job to do.

"I don't really know what to tell you, or how," Brandon said. "I was... upset. I guess that's the word."

"The night before they found your uncle, you mean?" asked Jasmine. Luffy let out a groan, sounding thoroughly unimpressed with her supposed subtlety.

Brandon nodded. "I wasn't at home. I didn't play any video games. I..."

He faltered then, his head hanging and his cheeks going even redder than usual. To console him, Jasmine reached out and grabbed his hand.

"You can tell me," she said quietly. "You can tell me anything, Brandon."

"It was about you," he replied, looking up at her.

"Me?"

He nodded. "I was... depressed, because I thought you would never say yes. I thought, if I finally plucked up the courage to ask, things would work out the way I always envisioned them. You and me together. It sounds stupid, I know, but..."

"No, it's perfectly fine!" Jasmine said. "It doesn't sound stupid, Brandon."

He nodded. "I went for a walk. A long one. I walked all over the Cove. I even thought about stealing that old canoe and going out, but I guess it wouldn't be stealing since no one knows who owns it."

Jasmine smiled. "It's a good thing you didn't. That thing would probably disintegrate the second you started paddling. Did you spend very long at the beach, then?"

He shrugged. "I was there for a little while."

"When?"

"I dunno, why does it matter?" Brandon asked.

Jasmine shrugged. "Just curious. Was it around midnight, maybe?"

He stared at her. He kept on staring until after the waitress had come to set their dessert down. She sensed the tension and hurried away.

"What?" Jasmine finally asked.

"Why are you asking me all this stuff?" Brandon asked.

Perhaps the moment had come. Jasmine could have come up with a lie, but lying was not in her nature. She was terrible at it. Besides, she had already come here with the intention of giving Brandon the truth.

So she took out Lustbader's note and slid it over. Thank goodness for that note; it kept on coming in handy, an easy way to get her point across without having to verbalize it herself.

"So you're investigating me?" Brandon asked, his voice strangely calm.

"Well... only sort of," Jasmine said.

He let out a dry laugh. A sound of disbelief. The hurt was plain in his eyes.

"Okay," he said. "Um... well... ask away. Whatever questions you have. It's alright."

"No, it isn't," Jasmine said, snatching the note back and stowing it away. "It's not OK. I don't know what I was thinking."

Brandon forced a smile onto his face. "No, it's alright. Go ahead. I don't mind."

Jasmine felt like locking herself into a cell and throwing the key where she couldn't reach it.

"I guess I'm not really investigating you," she said. "I just wanted to ask a few questions. I thought, if we were meeting anyway, I might as well tag a few on at the end."

Brandon nodded. He took a bite of his dessert, his arm moving mechanically. His eyes looked distant and dazed.

There was only one way out of this now. And that was through.

"You were at the beach that night," she said. "If you were at the docks, looking at that canoe, you were also pretty close to Jack's cottage."

Brandon nodded. "Yeah. Close enough. But I couldn't actually see it. All the lights were off."

"Did you see anything else, maybe? Another person nearby?

Did you hear anything?"

"I heard a motor," Brandon said. "Yeah. Like a motorboat. It was somewhere out in the water. Not like a speedboat, just a quiet kind of rumbling sound. But I didn't see anyone on the beach."

"What time was this?" Jasmine asked again.

"Probably one o'clock in the morning. Maybe even later. I dunno, I was just walking aimlessly. Like a zombie. I wasn't paying much attention to anything."

"How long were you walking for?"

"All night. Then the sun started coming up and I remembered I had a shift at the Nook. I thought there was no way I'd be any good that day, so I decided to trade shifts with you."

Jasmine nodded. "And now we're here."

"Yep," said Brandon. He took another bite of dessert. Slower this time. He glanced warily at Jasmine.

She made a show of eating her dessert as well, making a bit more casual conversation. It didn't flow at all like it had earlier. Brandon was guarded, answering in short sentences. He kept looking out the window, as the sea fog continued rolling in.

Meanwhile, the real questions were still percolating in Jasmine's mind. If she didn't ask them now, she might never find the strength later on.

"Brandon, this is going to sound ridiculous," she said. "But I need to hear it from you. Were you in your uncle's cottage that night? Did you visit him? Did you see him at all?"

At first Brandon shook his head, but then a disturbed look came to his face as he realized what she was actually asking.

"You think I might have *killed him?*" he asked, incredulous. "Are you serious?"

"No, I don't think you did," Jasmine said. "But I have to ask everyone the same—"

He interrupted her by slamming the table. Not with his fists but rather with his knees by accident, in his haste to stand up. His hands were shaking as he pulled a twenty dollar bill out of his pocket and dropped it in the middle of the table. After a moment, he added a ten and two ones.

"Your burger was nine bucks," he said. "My sandwich was seven. The desserts were six bucks apiece. That should cover everything. The tip, too."

He left, walking stiffly, his beat-up old shoes scuffing the floor several times. He had gone into hunchback mode again, a shrunken young man with a bruised heart.

Jasmine watched him go. And then she turned back to her dessert. She pushed the plate away. If she ate a single bite, she thought she would probably puke.

CHAPTER 7

"Brandon, it's me again. We need to talk. I want to apologize for how stupid I was. Please call me back."

Jasmine hung up and jammed her phone back in her pocket. She sighed as she looked back up at the world around her. The road sloping down through Blackwood Cove, toward the beach. The sky was overcast, and the wind that sliced through from the sea was bitter and edged with a damp cold that seemed to soak into her bones.

It had been two weeks since she had sat down with Brandon at the Spyglass Diner. Two weeks since she had done any investigative work at all. She had come to the conclusion that it had all been a huge, silly mistake. Just her overactive imagination trying to break free, making mountains out of mole hills.

Nowadays, as she floated between training appointments and work at the Nook, she was learning to be satisfied with the truth. The truth was rarely very flashy, or interesting. But it had its own merits. There was something noble in it. And Jasmine was trying to do as the rest of the townspeople did. When something bad happened, they didn't run around trying to figure out why. They just grumbled a few times, shrugged their shoulders, and got on with their daily lives.

Jasmine started walking. Luffy was close by, as always. They were on their way to nowhere in particular. Just getting some air. Life was boring now, even a bit suffocating. Nothing really changed from day to day other than the weather. It was getting colder now, winter was showing its ugly face, and the townspeople were spending less and less time outdoors. The Cove was falling asleep. And Jasmine felt like she was falling asleep as well, in a way. Falling under a spell, from which she would awake only when she finally got out of this town and went away to college.

There was nothing left for her here now.

When she was halfway down to the beach, her phone rang. She nearly dropped it into a sewer drain in her haste to get it out... but it was not Brandon's number that showed on the screen. She answered the call anyway.

"Hello?"

"Is this Jasmine Moore?" a vaguely familiar voice asked.

"Um... that depends on who I'm talking to."

"This is Julie Barnes, from the Cove Herald. I stopped in at the Nook a few days ago and Patrick Walker told me all about your investigation. I asked how I could get in touch with you, and he gave me your number. He said you wouldn't mind."

"Two weeks ago, I wouldn't have," Jasmine replied. Two weeks ago, she would have been giddy to receive a call from such a local celebrity.

"Oh. Well, in that case I'm sorry to have bothered you."

"No, don't be. It's alright. It's just that... well, I'm not doing the investigation anymore."

"Aren't you?" Julie asked, sounding genuinely crestfallen. "Well, that's too bad. Because my own investigation has slowed to less than a crawl. I was hoping we might be able to help each other out. We could compare notes. And when my story comes out about the life of Jack Torres, I'll be sure to give you credit. If you would like that."

Jasmine thought about it for a moment. Luffy looked up at her, curious. With his sharp canine hearing, he was no doubt listening in on the conversation.

"I don't think I have much to offer you," Jasmine said. "I hit the wall on my investigation a while ago."

"I'm sorry to hear that. Information does seem a little thin, doesn't it? I don't know that Jack was murdered, but there's definitely a story here. I hope you will reconsider in the future."

"I wouldn't count on it," said Jasmine. "Sorry."

"That's alright, Jasmine. You have a good day now, alright?"

"Thanks," Jasmine said, then ended the call.

"What are you, nuts?" Luffy asked.

"No, I'm saner than I have been in a long time," Jasmine replied. "If you hadn't noticed, I haven't had any more of those seizures lately. I guess they were probably stress-induced."

"But you're just as stressed as usual!" Luffy pressed.

Jasmine smiled, patting his flank. "My poor puppy just misses all the extra walks we were taking when my idiot self thought Jack had been murdered. Don't worry; we'll take an extra-long one today. How about we go down to the beach?"

That got a response. Luffy's front paws left the ground several times as he bounced excitedly. They continued down the sidewalk at a quicker pace, both to reach the beach sooner and to combat the cold.

**

The high temperature for the day was thirty-six degrees, but it was a few degrees cooler than that when Jasmine and Luffy reached the beach. She didn't expect to see anyone else, given the unforgiving conditions. But, as she took a narrow path down between two houses and stepped onto that expanse of gritty, gray sand, she was aware of another presence on the beach. She saw someone from the corner of her eye, far enough along that she couldn't make out any details about them.

At first she and Luffy went the opposite direction. They meandered along. Or rather, *she* meandered, idling at about two miles an hour. Meanwhile, Luffy ran in wide circles and figure-eights nearby, splashing through the surf and sprinting along, leaving footprints in the compressed sand that were gone by the time the next wave washed over them.

Jasmine was shivering by the time she reached the cliffs. She made her way warily up a field of increasingly larger boulders, the sea spray dashing across her face with each surging set of waves. Luffy watched her from the ground, tail wagging, barking nervously now and then. When he got really scared, he often forgot to communicate in their usual way.

"It's okay, I'll be fine," Jasmine called down. "I used to do this all the time as a kid."

She continued upward, testing each foot and handhold before placing any weight on it. It was impossible to find any ground that wasn't wet; she was mostly looking for sections of stone that weren't slick and slimy with algae.

Eventually, she reached a point where she could go no further. The cliff reared up before her, a sheer face of black stone filigreed with cracks and fissures, where little tufts of moss grew. She laid her hand against the cliff for support as she turned to face the sea. Narrowing her eyes to the wind, she stared toward the horizon.

If the weather had been nicer, she could have stayed up here forever. But the temperature was dropping, and now that Luffy had stopped running and was staring up at her in concern he was beginning to shiver. After one last look out into the ocean she turned back and began the climb down.

As she stretched her leg down to find a place for her foot, she glanced to the side and noticed that the lone figure she had seen further up the beach was coming closer. It was a man, dressed in a yellow rain coat, tall and broad shouldered. She couldn't tell anything else about his appearance, but still... there was something about him that made her pause and stare.

Her hand slipped. She fell, skidding roughly down the face of the boulder. Falling toward a crevice that was ten or twelve feet deep, and narrow enough to trap her. Thinking fast, she kicked and shoved off the boulder and launched herself to the next one over, clinging to it for dear life.

At first her heart was thumping so hard in her ears that she didn't hear Luffy's whining barks. She crawled to the edge of the boulder and looked down, wincing in pain from the scrapes and contusions to her hands and chest. Luffy was trying to climb up.

"It's alright," she said. "I'm fine."

Luffy stared up at her, licking his nose anxiously.

Further up the beach, the man in the raincoat was now on the run. He was sprinting toward her, flinging wet sand behind him. When she stood and gave him a halfhearted wave, he slowed his pace but did not turn around.

Adrenaline allowed her to make the climb down in no time at all. She landed back in the sand and finally took a look at her hands. There were flaps of loose skin everywhere, layers that had been shredded by the rough stone. The flesh over her sternum probably looked about the same. But she wasn't bleeding. And now that the shock had worn off, she felt foolish.

And embarrassed, too. She would have greatly preferred it if Luffy had been the only one to witness her clumsiness.

With a sigh, she turned to check the progress of the stranger. He was walking along, close enough now that she could see the amused smile on his face. He was sticking close to the water. In fact, he was close enough to it that each wave washed over his feet, soaking his tennis shoes, a fact which somehow didn't seem to bother him.

The next breath Jasmine drew caught in her throat for a moment as she realized she had seen this man before. But not with her eyes.

"I saw you fall," the man called out over the sound of the surf. "Are you alright?"

She nodded. "Yeah. I'm fine. Um... what...? Who...?"

"The name's Marlon," he said. "Marlon Gale. Pleased to meet you."

"Jasmine," she responded. "Um... this is Luffy."

The dog barked. He was at ease again now, seeming to smile as he glanced around lazily.

"Pleased to meet you too, Luffy," Marlon said, nodding at the dog. Then he looked back at Jasmine. "Well, if you aren't hurt, I guess we can both go back to our self-imposed isolation."

He started to turn away.

"Wait!" Jasmine said. "You don't live in Blackwood Cove, do

you?"

He turned back and shook his head. "I'm here to sightsee."

"It's almost winter," Jasmine noted. "There's not a lot going on around here anymore. Not until May."

Marlon shrugged. "Who said I wanted to be somewhere that has things going on? I don't mind the quiet. And I like to avoid crowds. I guess you probably understand that, since you're out here on your own too."

Luffy barked again.

"But I guess you're not on your own," Marlon corrected himself.

Jasmine gestured at his feet. "Your shoes..."

"Oh, yeah," he said, chuckling. "I stepped in a big old puddle on my way out here. I figured since my feet were already wet I might as well enjoy the water. I thought it might give me a deeper connection to this place."

"If you say so."

Marlon nodded. "I'll be on my way, then. If you're sure you don't need any help. That looked like it could have been a nasty fall."

"No, I'm fine," said Jasmine. "Promise."

He turned to leave. And Jasmine could think of nothing else to say, so she just watched him go. A few minutes later, she and Luffy headed up the beach in his wake.

"You buying that crap story of his?" Luffy asked. "Sightseeing in the Cove when winter is right around the corner?"

"No," said Jasmine. "But there's something else. That man..."

"Marlon Gale," Luffy repeated. "He seemed nice."

"He seemed *familiar.* Luffy, that was the guy I saw in my vision. The guy on the beach with the wet shoes!"

The dog looked up at her. "Are you sure?"

"Positive! He was black, he was the right age, and he was wearing a raincoat. It was the same exact person, Luffy."

They walked along in silence for a long moment. To one side was the sea, frothing and lapping at the sand. To the other side was the tall, yellow scrub grass that grew at the edge of town.

Deep in the heart of it they could see the ruins of an old shed, collapsing in on itself.

"What does this mean?" Luffy asked.

"It means my visions were predicting the future," Jasmine said simply.

"Doesn't that seem a little...?"

"Farfetched?" she said.

Luffy's ears perked up. "Fetch? Sure, let's play!"

Jasmine smiled. "No, you goof! I mean... well, it might sound ridiculous and impossible, but I would say this means I can see the future. In a limited way. It's the only explanation I can come up with. It's not like I had a hazy dream and now my mind is filling in the blanks. I actually saw this Marlon guy. I even wrote it down! Luffy, this is crazy."

"You can say that again. Is there some other explanation?"

"Not that I can think of," said Jasmine. "You heard the guy. He's not from the Cove. I've never seen him before, and I'll bet no one else in town has either. So it's not like I subconsciously remembered him from somewhere."

"Okay," said Luffy. "My friend Jasmine can talk to her dog. She also has seizures and can see the future."

"Only a few seconds of it," she added. "And I can't control what I see."

"Is it just me, or is this a little scary? I'm worried, Jasmine."

"Why? This is awesome! It means I wasn't actually having seizures. Not really. I was just getting... I dunno, messages."

"From who?" Luffy asked suspiciously.

"I dunno. From no one probably. Who knows how or why this is happening? I once read a science fiction book where a future scientist was communicating with a past one by encoding messages inside particles called tachyons."

"You lost me."

"All I mean is, there's got to be some scientific reason for all this. I'm not a witch."

"I never said you were," Luffy said. "But we can drown you in the river just to make sure."

"Not funny."

"It's a *little* funny. But anyway, does this mean that all the other things you saw are going to come true as well?"

"If they haven't already," Jasmine said, nodding.

***

The two of them rushed home as fast as possible. They tore up the stairs and into Jasmine's room, where she dug out her notes and went back through them.

"Someone is in trouble for something they did," Jasmine read from the first vision. "Their shoes are wet, leaving footprints."

"And then the grocery store ends up closing for the first day in history," Luffy added. "That was the second one, right?"

Jasmine nodded. "And then I saw Jack's cottage. The front door was open, and I saw Brandon sneaking around nearby."

"And then... was it Cynthia and Patrick?"

"Yup. Fighting in the bookstore. The fifth vision was the guy we just saw, Marlon Gale. Here, let me write his name down..."

She grabbed a pen and did so. Then she cut out the notes with a pair of scissors and attached them to the wall with a piece of tape.

"There haven't been any visions for two weeks," she said. "Ever since I stopped investigating. These five clues may be all we get. *May* be."

"If they even are clues," Luffy reminded her. "We just met this Marlon guy, and I highly doubt he has anything to do with Jack's death."

Jasmine shrugged. "These visions started accelerating as soon as I began digging around. And they stopped as soon as I also stopped. That can't be a coincidence. I hope you're ready Luffy, because I think the visions are going to start up again."

"Huh? How come?"

She answered him by pulling out her phone and dialing back the most recent incoming call.

"Cove Herald, Julie Barnes speaking," a voice answered immediately.

"Hi, Julie. It's Jasmine Moore."

"Jasmine! I had a feeling you would call back."

"What kind of feeling?" Jasmine asked.

"Just that you wouldn't be able to give up so easily."

"Oh. I guess your feeling was correct. I know this probably seems like an abrupt turnaround, but... does your offer still stand?"

"Yes, of course! I'm here at the Herald office until six today. Stop in any time. I'll be waiting for you. With bated breath!"

"I'll be there soon," Jasmine promised. "One more thing..."

"Yes?"

"Can I bring my dog Luffy inside?"

***

The Cove Herald occupied an unassuming brick building on the corner of Main and Duke. It had a bike lock out front, a bench, and a small shade tree... not that shade was much required in the Cove.

Luffy and Jasmine went inside and felt a wash of furnace heat down the back of their necks as they stepped through the vestibule. They entered a small and tidy waiting area, where a secretary glanced up and smiled, waving them through.

"Julie's in the office at the end," the helpful woman said.

Jasmine nodded and stepped through a doorway. She found herself in a short hallway with three doors along the wall. One was labeled SUPPLIES. The other two bore the names of two other contributors to the paper, neither of whom seemed to be in residence. Perhaps they were only part time workers. The Cove Herald was a weekly paper, and it was often quite slim. There was rarely anything worth writing about, and the staff often had to scrape the bottom of the barrel.

The door at the end of the hall was marked JULIE BARNES - EDITOR. Jasmine knocked at it.

"Come in!" a chipper voice called out.

They stepped through and Jasmine shut the door behind them. Immediately she was struck with a powerful flowery scent. There were plants everywhere, covering every available surface. Branches and leaves draped over the edge of every bit of furniture. The effect was as if Julie had carved out a bit of office space in an unruly jungle, and her desk already seemed to be growing over with vines.

As far as the desk itself went, it was sparse. Julie had a laptop, with a charging cable snaking across the surface of the desk. There was a wireless mouse on a pad, a cup of coffee on a coaster, and a neat stack of pages; probably articles waiting to be proofed. And that was all.

"Jasmine!" the editor said, standing up to reach across the table. She was a tall woman with hair that somewhat resembled a blond waterfall.

Jasmine shook hands with her. "Thanks for inviting me, Julie. I've actually always wanted to come in here."

"Into the Herald?" Julie asked, sitting back down, which was Jasmine's cue to do the same. "Is it everything you dreamt it would be?"

"It's small," Jasmine admitted.

"And so is our staff. I think we're sized perfectly. Can I get you anything, by the way? Something to drink?'

"I'm fine for now."

"Then we can get to why we're both here. I should be at home right now... there's nothing left to do that I can't do from the comfort of my armchair. Or better yet, my bathtub. But I was just certain you would call back. And here you are!"

Jasmine nodded. "So, you don't think Jack's death was an accident?"

Julie smiled. "To tell you the truth, Jasmine, I don't really think or believe anything specific. I always try to remain... unbiased, I suppose is the right word. However, I'm open to any possibility, and either way this is going to be a good story. The best we've had in years."

"Decades, maybe?" Jasmine suggested with a grin.

Julie chuckled. "Maybe. But let's not dwell on the past. I would like to hear everything you've managed to gather, Jasmine."

"And then you'll tell me everything that you know?"

"Of course." Julie gestured at her computer. "I have my notes pulled up. As you speak, I can strike out anything that we've both discovered. That way I can give you just the things that are new."

Jasmine nodded and launched into it. She started off at the very beginning, marching into the police station and talking to Sheriff Lustbader. And she ended on today, seeing the mysterious stranger on the beach.

"Marlon Gale," Julie said. "I've never heard that name before. But if there's a stranger in town, I'm sure I'll hear about it from someone else by the end of the day. From Marsha Cargill, at least."

"Did you hear anything else new?" Jasmine asked. She noticed that Julie hadn't touched her computer much.

"It seems as though we've identified mostly the same information independently," Julie said. "However, due to the advantages of my post, I have slightly expanded knowledge. For instance, I've known about Jack's attacks on the character of Randy Ballard for years. Jack once came to me and asked if I would help him investigate Randy, because the police wouldn't touch the matter."

"I wonder why," Luffy said.

"Also," Julie went on, "I overheard Ruby Evans at the grocery store a while back... in March, I think it was. She was speaking with one of her friends about an incident between her and Jack. She didn't go into any fine details on what happened, but I gathered that it was something rather bitter and nasty. While you were talking with Ruby, did you get the impression that she had fallen out with him?"

"I thought that everyone had fallen out with Jack," said Jasmine.

Julie shook her head. "I mean that Ruby stopped doing her neighborly duty and bringing him treats on Holidays. She didn't visit him at all last year."

"How do you know that?" Jasmine asked.

"I have my sources, and you don't need to know all of them. We'll trust each other, Jasmine. If you have any information that may be... sensitive, or with a source that you cannot disclose, my ears are open."

Jasmine looked down at Luffy. He looked back up at her, tilting his head.

"What's the worst that could happen?" he asked.

"There is something, maybe," Jasmine said, looking back at Julie. "I heard that maybe Cynthia Jackson and Patrick Walker have some sort of strained relationship."

Julie smiled. "Yes, you could say that. It's interesting you've brought this up, Jasmine, because it involves Jack as well."

"It does?"

"Yes. It's not something anyone really talks about... but a long time back, in their middle school days in fact, Jack and Patrick were good friends."

"You're kidding!"

"I'm not. I think Patrick was the only friend Jack ever had. They were inseparable for a while. But it all went downhill."

"Why?"

"Because of Cynthia Jackson," Julie said.

"How?" Jasmine asked. "She's such a nice woman, I can't believe she could ever..."

"It wasn't anything she did or even said. It was just children being foolish. You see, Jack and Patrick had both fallen in puppy love with her. Just like every other boy in school, probably. And while I don't think Cynthia ever felt the same way about either of them, she tended to get along better with Patrick. Soon enough the two of them became closer friends. It was too much for Jack to handle, and he withdrew. From everything. He had always been a quiet boy, to himself, but I think his unrequited love for Cynthia was the catalyst that turned him into the man he became."

"Everyone has crushes in school," Jasmine said, "and they almost never amount to anything. So what?"

"It wasn't just the crush. It was the loss of his friendship with Patrick. Jack felt like he had been betrayed. And he kept that feeling for his entire life. I think it was one of the reasons he never allowed himself to get close to anyone, or for anyone to get close to him. Deep down, I believe Jack had a lot of good in him. But he never stopped trying to kill it. He thought it was a weakness."

Jasmine stared at the wall in shock. "I never knew any of this."

"The only reason I know it is because I was around to see it happen," Julie replied. "Neither Cynthia nor Patrick will ever bring it up. But the story doesn't end at middle school. Patrick eventually moved on from her, as far as I know, but Jack never did. He loved Cynthia until the day he died. He tried to kill every last connection to the people around him, but that was the one thread that he couldn't sever. Things calmed down a bit during those years when Cynthia was away doing her modeling across the world. But when she finally came back and settled in the Cove again, it started back up."

"What did?" Jasmine asked.

"The harassment. Randy wasn't the only one that Jack bothered habitually. He also had it out for your boss. Patrick eventually got a restraining order, but that only stopped Jack from entering his place of work. The last altercation I know of happened in the commons one day, with Jack following Patrick around and shouting what a terrible person and friend he was."

Jasmine shook her head. "This is…"

"I know," said Julie, reaching across to pat the younger woman's hand. "It's a lot to take in. I don't envy your youth, Jasmine. You're just as smart as the rest of us, but you're still treated as a child. If you want to be seen as a serious investigator, and get the real answers, you must be firm from now on. Don't take no for an answer. Assert yourself. I first started writing for the Herald when I was sixteen. The editor who worked here before me used to run my pieces as part of a column called 'kiddy corner.' Not very flattering. But look at me now… I took his job. After he retired, of course."

"Thanks, Julie," Jasmine said. "I'll try harder."

"You've done very well already, Jasmine. You've begun to uncover the truth about things around Blackwood Cove. You've begun to dig up old secrets. And, if Jack really was murdered, it's likely that one or more of those secrets has something to do with it. Keep going."

Jasmine nodded, feeling brave. "I will. Definitely."

"And you'll keep checking in with me?"

"As long as you keep telling me what you know," Jasmine replied.

"Of course. Fair is fair. There is one more thing I'd like to talk to you about right now. The mayor and his wife."

"What about them?" Jasmine asked.

"Well, let's just say that Jack Torres has long been seen as a stain on an otherwise idealistic New England tourist destination. Crazy Jack, as they call him, has been known to occasionally harass tourists, scaring them away from the beach and souring their view of the town. It seems to me that the two people who run this entire place might have seen him as a problem."

"I understand. But Eugene... he seems like a really nice guy."

"Yes, he sure does," said Julie. "He may just be the mayor of a small town, Jasmine, but he's still a politician. I think he does care about the Cove very much, perhaps even more than I do. I've known Eugene Carter for most of my life, and I understand his character. He's always been a man who is unafraid to attack an issue head on."

Jasmine nodded slowly, trying to soak all this in. "You mentioned his wife, too."

Julie settled back in her chair. "Ah, Laura Carter. Where do I begin? Whereas Cynthia had the looks, Laura had the smarts. She's always had a way of wiggling herself into exactly the position she wants. She even stole Homecoming Queen from Cynthia one year, which in retrospect is simply unbelievable. Laura isn't ugly, but how do you compare to perfection?"

"So, you think Laura could have killed Jack?"

"She could have. She also could have found a way to have him killed using an outside party. Who knows? The point is, that woman is a cross between a leech and a chameleon. I don't think anyone knows who she really is. Not even her husband."

"What about their kids?" Jasmine asked.

Julie waved a hand and made a sour face. "The two of them are just like their mother. Believe me. They live on the other side of the country, and good luck getting them to answer your calls. Forget about them. I highly doubt they know anything about what went on here. They forgot about Blackwood Cove as soon as they left it."

The editor took a drink of coffee, staring thoughtfully at Jasmine over the rim of the cup.

"One more thing about Laura that may be of interest," she said, setting the cup down. "But of course, you already know."

"Know what?"

"The connection. As far as I know Laura and Jack never shared so much as a single word... but they have something in common."

"Sailing," Jasmine said.

Julie nodded. "She goes out on that little yacht of hers every chance she has, and she almost never brings anyone with her. Who knows what she gets up to out there?"

Jasmine shrugged. She didn't see that there was much of anything to get up to on a boat, other than fishing or catching a bit of sun.

But still, the connection was there. Jack and Laura both sailed out of the same harbor, and they were both avid in their hobby. It stood to reason that they would have crossed paths on numerous occasions. They may even have spoken a number of times, alone on the dock. It was enough to make Laura Carter a suspect.

Jasmine thought about telling Julie all of this. But of course, the editor already would have thought of it. Julie had been ahead of her the whole time... but it seemed now they were at last on an even keel.

"I guess we need to talk to Laura," Jasmine said.

"And that's where the issues crop up," said Julie. "I've already tried getting hold of Laura and Eugene. Each time I call the house, one of their staff answers. Usually the maid. And the excuses are always the same; Eugene can't come to the phone right now, he's in a meeting. Laura can't come to the phone right now... blah, blah. I did manage to corner Eugene at the Shoppe Right a few days ago, but he sidestepped all my questions. Those two aren't going to give us an inch; we'll have to find a way to take it."

"How?" Jasmine asked.

Julie shrugged. "I don't know yet. But if I think of something, I'll call you. You do the same."

Jasmine nodded. "I will."

"Good. Thank you very much, Jasmine. I can already tell this is going to be a mutually beneficial partnership."

That seemed to be Jasmine's cue to leave. She stood up and shook hands with Julie.

"Is there anything I should be doing, specifically?" she asked.

"Follow your gut," Julie replied. "It will almost always lead you to fruitful pastures."

Jasmine nodded, turning to leave with Luffy right behind her.

"Oh, one last thing," Julie said. "This boy, Brandon Watson... Jack's nephew."

Jasmine looked back.

"Do you really think he might have murdered his uncle?" Julie asked.

"I don't want to say yes," Jasmine said. "But I just don't know."

CHAPTER 8

The investigation was back on, and Jasmine decided to plow full steam ahead.

She had a shift at the Book Nook the very next day, and she wished she had a time machine so she could get there right this second. She had questions for Patrick, questions that burned. She just hoped they wouldn't burn any bridges.

For now, there wasn't a huge amount she could do. She could possibly go back to Ruby's house and try and dig for what had gone on between her and Jack... except it was only four o'clock and the woman wouldn't be home from work yet. She could try and find Brandon, pay him a visit at home, but such a visit had no bearing on her investigation. She had no further questions for him at this point, and the only reason she had for finding him was to try and assuage some of her guilt.

Which *was* something she knew she must do at some point. Unless, of course, it turned out that Brandon had done the unthinkable. In that case, she would be absolved.

What else was there? She had gleaned everything she could from Randy Ballard for now. And if Laura and Eugene Carter were giving the slip to their very own Julie Barnes, it was highly doubtful they would humor the efforts of a teenager.

She expressed all this aloud to Luffy as they walked back down Main Street, leaving the Herald behind.

"It's alright," Luffy said. "You'll be twenty in a couple of months."

She had to laugh at that.

"My age isn't the main concern," she told him. "It's the fact that I'm probably going to have to waste the rest of the day. There's nothing to do!"

"Sure there is," said Luffy. "What is it that cops are always doing in those shows you watch? They go to the scene of the crime and stare off into space wistfully. Trying to get in the head of the killer, or whatever."

Jasmine shrugged. "I guess it's something."

The beach, then, became their next destination.

As they were crossing Main Street, a familiar and despairing sight was revealed to them. A cherry red convertible, parked up on the road outside the barbershop. Jasmine quickened her pace, hoping to avoid the driver of that car altogether, but fate had a different plan.

Just as they passed in front of the barbershop, the door opened and Barry Brock stepped out, looking trim with his fresh haircut. He smiled down at Jasmine as he pulled on a pair of sleek leather gloves.

"Good afternoon, Ms. Moore," he said. "And to you, Luffy. Still running around without a leash, I see. What gives?"

"What gives is that I'm the best-behaved dog in town," Luffy said. "But I'll still bite your nose off, you sorry sack of-"

He stopped when Jasmine lay a hand on his head.

"Luffy doesn't stray," she said. "He doesn't need a leash."

"My dear child," said Barry, "any dog will stray under the right circumstance. Let's see... a fun looking squirrel darts out from under a parked car. Your furry friend decides to chase it, and runs out into the road just in time to be struck by a pickup truck moving at a very ill-advised thirty miles an hour. What then?"

"Not going to happen," Jasmine replied.

"Oh, sure. That's what I thought too, until the day after my ninth birthday when the scenario I just described happened to my very own yellow Labrador, a beautiful girl named Lula. I learned a valuable lesson that day, Jasmine. And today it seems I have learnt another one. Sometimes it is not the dog that requires training, but rather the owner."

"Sorry, Jasmine," Luffy said with a deep, throaty growl, "but I think you're going to be solving a murder a lot sooner than you thought. I'll show him what an unleashed dog can do."

"No!" Jasmine said quickly, tapping the side of Luffy's snout.

Barry smirked as he pulled on his second glove and pulled out his car keys. "Unleashed and potentially vicious. I'll remember this. And *you*, girl, will remember that I have quite a bit more authority around here than you do. Now back away so that I may reach my car in safety."

Jasmine's heart thudded, her veins running with venom, but she did as he asked. Barry stepped down from the barbershop steps and approached his car. He hit a button to unlock it.

"Wait," Jasmine said.

Barry gave her a surprised look over his shoulder. But he did wait, impatiently tapping his foot. By the smug expression on his face, it seemed he was expecting a profuse apology.

"Can you tell me anything about Jack Torres?" Jasmine asked.

The question took Barry completely by storm. He reacted to it viscerally, a full body shiver passing over him.

"Don't ever mention that name to me again," he said.

Without another word he jumped into his car and was off, tires screeching on the pavement.

"What was that all about?" Luffy asked.

"I dunno. Could be nothing. Or it could be something. Either way, we aren't getting any answers from *that* idiot."

They resumed their walk, headed for the beach.

"I liked that part," Luffy said after a moment.

Jasmine gave him a funny look. "Which part?"

"The part where you called him an idiot. I think you really hit the nail on the head with that one."

Perhaps an idiot had gotten away with murder, Jasmine thought.

Barry Brock was at the forefront of her thoughts as she made her way to the beach. She finally came back to reality as her feet fell into the gritty sand; it made a slushing sound beneath her as she headed in the direction of Jack's Cottage.

Technically, the building could be reached by a pathway that wound down from Bristol Lane. But the sand was nicer. And it was a longer trek; it gave her more time to think.

The entirety of Bristol Lane was paralleled by a rough stone retaining wall near the beach, a sort of breakwater that protected the town from all but the rarest storm waves. Jasmine clung to it, running her sore and battered hand along the edges of the stone barrier. As she came around one curved end of the wall, she found herself within view of Jack's cottage. It was a small structure, hunkered down beneath an algae-coated tin roof. It hung above the sand on salt and barnacle encrusted wooden stilts; underneath it, in the cold shadows, she saw a few tiny crabs waltzing around in their own private, miniature lagoon.

Jack's cottage wasn't alone. Not far away, further up the beach and sitting in the scrub grass, was another dwelling of similar size. This was the one occupied by Donald Parks, one of the Cove's African American residents. He was the type of hermit everyone wished Jack would have been. Quiet and polite, always friendly.

Jasmine walked up the beach and around onto the walkway in front of Jack's cottage. She approached the door and peeked through a tiny window; it was all darkness and silence inside. With the cat gone, the only life here now was the sad little crabs down below.

"It's strange, what happened," a voice came from behind her, so soft that she didn't even jump.

She turned and saw a black man walking toward her. At first she thought it was Marlon Gale again, but then she saw the gray hair under the hood the man was wearing. This was Donald Parks, clinging to a stack of mail. He must have been on his way back from his mailbox when he saw her down here.

"Yes," said Jasmine. "Strange."

Donald nodded slowly, drumming on his leg with his free hand. It seemed he had something he wanted to say, and was trying to find the right words. Or summon the courage.

"Oh," he said, as though something had only just occurred to him. "You're that girl, aren't you? The one who's investigating?"

"That's me," Jasmine replied. "But I only just started back up again today."

"That's good." Donald nodded again. "Say, I may have something you'd like to hear."

Jasmine quickly hauled out her phone. "Of course! Do you mind if I record?"

Donald shook his head, then watched patiently as she used her cold, numb hands to work her phone. When she gave him the go ahead, he continued.

"It was just something I happened to overhear," he began. "It was on Thanksgiving two years ago. I had burnt the pie I was baking so I opened the windows to clear out the smoke. Otherwise I wouldn't have heard it."

"What did you hear?"

"Fighting. Loud arguing. A man and a woman screaming at each other. I knew the one voice belonged to Jack. We never spoke except a few words at the mail box or on the beach, but when you live close to someone for all those years you definitely recognize their voice."

"Who was the other person?" Jasmine asked, though she already knew.

"I don't know her name, but I've seen her around. She's short and wears her hair in a ponytail. Dark hair. In fact she's dark all around. Maybe she has native blood, I don't know."

It sounded like Ruby to a T.

"I've seen her around, alright," Donald went on. "Every year during the holidays. But this time I guess she and Jack got into it. I watched her storm out of his house and back up to Bristol with what looked like a full plate of food in her hand. All wrapped in foil."

And that *also* sounded like Ruby.

"Did you hear anything specific that they were saying?" Jasmine asked.

At first Donald shook his head, but then he remembered something.

"I think I heard a few words from the lady. 'Don't you dare.' Something like that. That's all I got. Sorry if I wasn't much help, I've just been a bit worried since last year when I didn't see the lady come back. I thought you might want to know."

"Yes, this is very helpful," she said, stopping the recording. "Thanks, Mr. Parks."

He nodded and turned away without saying anything else, carrying his mail home.

Jasmine walked a few slow circuits around Jack's cottage, mulling over the things she had learned today. Her case, or whatever she was calling it, had suddenly grown by leaps and bounds. There was so much information to keep track of, so many variables and potential clues, that she had no idea where to go next.

It was on her third lap around, just as she was passing Jack's front door again, when she realized Luffy was no longer with her.

She spoke his name, turning around. She expected to see him rounding the corner right behind her. But a moment passed, and he didn't appear.

She called his name more loudly. Still nothing.

The things Barry Brock had said flashed through her mind as she ran back around the corner of the house, expecting the worst. She didn't know what could possibly happen to a dog on an empty beach, but that didn't stop the cold fear from spreading through her.

A rare sight met her eyes. It was uncommon for Luffy to give in to the canine urge to dig holes, but that was what he was doing now. He was pawing furiously at the sand, throwing it in great plumes behind him. He had already gone about a foot down. The sand coming out was heavy and dark with moisture. Luffy showed no signs of stopping. When she ran over to see what he was up to, he glanced briefly at her with his nose covered in sand.

"What are you doing?" she asked. "What's gotten into you?"

"A *smell*, Jasmine," he replied in a frantic tone. "I got a smell! Something is buried right here, I know it..."

He kept on digging, breathing heavily and occasionally hacking in the cold air. Jasmine stood by and looked around, half anxious and half embarrassed. It probably wasn't the best look, letting her dog go crazy on a dead man's property. She was just waiting for Barry Brock to show up and make some haughty remark.

Suddenly, the noise coming from Luffy's hole changed. Before it had been the sighing, rasping sound of wet sand. And now there was something else, a plasticky crinkling.

"Got it!" Luffy announced proudly. He backed out of the hole, clasping a huge plastic bag in his jaw.

Jasmine took it from him and glanced around again, making sure they hadn't been witnessed. Then she turned to the hole and started kicking sand back into it.

"Good idea!" said Luffy. He turned around and began to help her.

"Wait!" said Jasmine. "We'll probably want to remember where this was buried. Whatever it is..."

Once the hole had been filled in again, she found a few rocks and arranged them in a conspicuous pattern on the sand. Then she paced out the distance from that spot to the corner of Jack's house, and told Luffy the number as well. If someone moved the rocks, she would still be able to find the right spot. Once that was finished, she beckoned Luffy and hurried up onto Bristol Lane.

Only then did she take a good look at what Luffy had unearthed. It didn't look like much; a few sheets of paper sealed in a bag. But she was willing to bet they contained some sort of useful information. Something vital. Otherwise, why bury them?

"I think we really found something here," she said as she stepped around the corner of a house, feeling giddy. "Luffy... I don't want to jinx it, but I think we're getting somewhere for sure!"

She realized someone was on the sidewalk ahead of her just in time to avoid crashing straight into them. She let out a surprised sound and quickly stepped to the side. The man in front of her reached out, resting a steadying hand briefly on her arm.

It was Marlon Gale. He wasn't wearing a raincoat today, but rather a cozy looking pea coat and a tartan scarf.

"Is it just me," he said, "or are you the most accident-prone person in Blackwood Cove?"

"I might be," she replied, smiling anxiously.

"It's Jasmine, right?" Marlon asked.

She nodded. "And you're Marlon Gale. Still walking around in the cold, I see?"

"Yup. It's invigorating, isn't it?"

"Um... sure."

Marlon gestured at the plastic bag. "What have you got there? Some kind of paperwork?"

"Uh... yeah. I thought it was going to rain, so I wanted to make sure it stayed dry."

"Okay," he said. She could tell he didn't believe a single thing she said, but he didn't press her further. Which was good, because he had no right to. She wasn't the only one sneaking around and making up lies.

"Going for another walk on the beach?" she asked, raising an eyebrow to tell him just what she thought of his story.

"Something like that," he replied. "I like the sound of the waves."

It was just vague enough not to be a lie.

She and Marlon parted ways. Jasmine continued along the sidewalk a few steps, then glanced back just in time to watch Marlon disappear down the same side path she had used, headed for the beach.

Or maybe someplace else.

"Luffy, do me a favor," she said.

"I'm all ears," he said, looking up at her. "And nose. And mouth. And tail."

"Well, I'll just need your feet and your eyes for this one. Why don't you go back down toward Jack's house. Slowly. Then come back and tell me what you see."

"I'm on it!"

Luffy sped off, remembered her request, then decelerated to a slow walk. Jasmine waited, pretending to be doing something on her phone.

The dog returned a few minutes later, looking excited.

"I saw him!" Luffy announced. "Marlon Gale!"

"Yeah? What was he doing?" Jasmine asked.

"The same thing we were! Walking around Jack's house in a circle. But then he saw me."

"What did he do?"

"He just sort of smiled and waved, then stared over my head. Like he was watching for something…"

"He was watching for me," Jasmine said. "What happened next?"

"He walked down to the beach. I waited a little bit but he didn't come back."

She gave him a scratch behind the ears. "Good work! I'll give you a nice big treat when we get home. There's probably some leftover meatloaf that's so old not even dad will eat it."

Luffy barked, even more excited than before.

***

It finally happened again as Jasmine was walking up the front steps of her house. She quickly lowered herself to the deck and leaned against the railing, waiting for the moment to pass.

When it did, she had a new image fresh in her mind's eyes. She told it to Luffy immediately so that it wouldn't be forgotten.

"It was Julie Barnes," she said. "I only saw her from the back, but she was too tall and blond to be anyone else."

"What else?" Luffy asked.

"She was holding something…"

"What was it? Did you see?"

"A picture. An old, faded photograph. There were two people in it. One of them was definitely Julie. She was young, probably not much older than I am. The other person…"

"Who?" Luffy asked. "Hurry up and tell me, before it slips away."

"I can't be sure. But it looked like it may have been Jack Torres."

***

Jasmine was feeling weak from her vision, but still buzzing with excitement as she climbed the steps to her room. She didn't feel like her case was very close to coming together, but there was now a distinct feeling of progress. She was getting to the bottom of something. She could feel it, just like Luffy could smell whatever it was he had dug out from under Jack's property.

She waited until she was behind her door, safe from the world, then she pulled an old blanket out of her closet and spread it on the floor. She set the plastic bag on top and stared at it for a long moment. There was a certain reverence and awe in that moment, as though she was staring down at a priceless historical artifact. Something that was older than the entire civilization she lived in.

Finally, she donned a pair of disposable plastic gloves and opened the bag. She was very careful as she removed the pages. She didn't know how old they might be.

It turned out they were in great shape, not faded or brittle at all. They looked to have been printed out very recently, probably in the past year or two.

That in itself was somewhat interesting. But as Jasmine began to read, she soon forgot about everything else.

She sat back, breathing heavily, shaking her head.

"I don't believe it," she said. "Jack was telling the truth."

"What do you mean?" Luffy asked, antsy and impatient. "What does it say?"

Jasmine quickly but gently pushed the pages back into the bag. She resealed it, tore off her gloves, and stood up with the bag under her arm.

She was in over her head. It was time to pay Sheriff Lustbader another visit.

***

"Are you sure you didn't open it?" Lustbader asked for the

third time.

They were in a conference room at the station this time. Jasmine was sitting in one chair of a dozen around a large oval table, her knees drawn up to her chest and Luffy hiding under the table in front of her.

She was being watched. Not just by the three officers who worked here full time, but also by an older man in a lab coat and thick glasses. His nametag announced him as Dr. Reynolds, and he had just arrived from the closest major city in a record-breaking hour and ten minutes.

"Well, just hypothetically speaking," Jasmine began. "If I *had* opened it, using the correct procedure with gloves and stuff..."

"We just need to know if the evidence has been contaminated," Dr. Reynolds said. He had been standing ever since he had arrived, humming with energy like a livewire, and he had already polished off several cups of coffee.

"Contaminated with what?" Jasmine asked.

"Anything," said Dr. Reynolds, and began ticking off items on his fingers. "Hair. Sweat. Skin. Skin oils. Blood. Saliva. Any of those things could have entered this bag from your body if you had opened it. Now it is sealed and presented as evidence. You understand how our data could become... confused."

"Couldn't we just test her and match her DNA against anything we find?" Lustbader asked with a sigh.

"Yes. That is exactly what we will have to do, Sheriff. However, what will this tell us? It will tell us that the DNA of Jasmine Moore was inside a sealed bag that was buried outside a dead man's house. That is *all* it will tell us. As for whether the bag was indeed from that area, we can confirm that by soil comparison quite easily."

"What are you saying?" Lustbader asked.

"I'm saying that if her DNA is found inside the bag, I will have no choice but to consider her a suspect in the death of Jack Torres... or at the very least as an accomplice in whatever dirty dealings that are described by the contents of this bag."

"Well," said Lustbader with a grunt, "it's a good thing this is my investigation, then, and not yours. This is ridiculous, Doctor. I didn't call you here to tell me who my suspects are."

Dr. Reynolds finally sat, affecting the posture of someone who was not prepared to move anytime soon. "Then why did you call me, Sheriff? Certainly it wasn't for the pleasure of my company. And as I recall, Jack's death is still being ruled an accident."

"So far that hasn't changed," Lustbader replied. "I called you here, Dr. Reynolds, because you're an expert. Not just in DNA, but in other things. You can test these documents. Check them out. Maybe send copies to your lab in the city."

"You would like me to confirm their validity," said Dr. Reynolds.

Lustbader nodded. "I haven't gotten this far in life by going off half-cocked. If I'm going to make any kind of move, I need to know for certain that it's going to be a good one."

"Sheriff," Dr. Reynolds said, smiling, "that's the smartest thing you've said to me so far. But are you sure it's a good idea to be discussing these things with Ms. Moore present?"

Lustbader laid a hand on Jasmine's shoulder. "She's one of my deputies, and she's done more work on this case than anyone else. She stays."

"How endearing," said Dr. Reynolds. "So, you're calling this a murder investigation now?"

"No. But I'm open to the possibility."

"Very well. I'll get to work, then, in the generous accommodations your station has provided to me. I should have some results by tomorrow afternoon. Early evening, perhaps."

"Thank you, Doctor," Lustbader said. "Now if all of you don't mind, I'd like a word with Jasmine alone. And with Luffy too, of course."

They all took the hint and filed out of the room. The door shut, and it was just the three of them. The Sheriff took a seat across the table from Jasmine and let out a long sigh.

"What a day," he said.

"Yup," Jasmine agreed.

"If Reynolds comes up with a positive result, Jasmine, I'm

going to have to arrest one of my fellow townspeople under suspicion of murder. I didn't think something like this could ever happen in Blackwood Cove."

"Me neither," Jasmine said. "I guess it goes to show that the crazy hermit might actually know what he's talking about sometimes."

Lustbader shook his head. "I can hardly believe it. Randy Ballard, of all people. The guy has always struck me as one of the straightest shooters around. And that's in a town full of nothing but straight shooters. But I can't deny what I saw in those pages. His books were so cooked it's a wonder he... Well, I've got nothing. My brain's so fried I can't even think of a decent analogy."

"I've got one," Luffy piped up. "His books were so cooked not even Luffy would eat them!"

Jasmine stifled a laugh, turning it into a cough in her hand.

"He was a fraud this whole time," Lustbader went on. "Even if I arrest him, it's just a matter of who tries to grab him from me first, the FBI or the IRS. I don't know how, but I guess Jack figured it out. And I think I know exactly how all this went down."

"So do I," said Jasmine. "Jack only had suspicions at first. He tried to draw the town's attention to what Randy was doing, but it was like the boy who cried wolf. No one trusted Jack, which made Randy look even more innocent than he was before. Jack started to get desperate. Angry that no one was listening to him. So he dug deeper. He finally got some real evidence, and he hid it in a safe spot. He tried to blackmail Randy with it, and... well, Randy found a way to shut him up. Is that about right?"

"Yep," Lustbader said. "That's the way I see it. It all sort of makes sense, doesn't it? In a sad kind of way."

"So," said Jasmine.

"So," Lustbader replied.

"What do we do next?"

"Well..." Lustbader stood up, stretching his arms over his head. "I'm going to get myself another cup of joe, and go digging through some old files. But I think you've done enough work for one day, Deputy Moore. Go ahead and knock off. Head home. Make sure your folks know everything's fine. I'll give you a call once I know something else."

She stood up. Lustbader walked all the way around the table and gave her a firm handshake.

"Good work," he said. "I know you want to go to the college and do whatever, but I think you could have a future in law enforcement."

His statement stuck with her all the way home. She somehow felt more confused than ever. It seemed her investigation was over almost as soon as it had begun, and now she had a sad and sinking feeling.

In the morning, there would be nothing for her to do but return to the humdrum of everyday life.

CHAPTER 9

She woke up with Brandon Watson on her mind. Now that the problem of who killed Jack Torres seemed to be solved, her anxious and hyperactive mind had turned to the next largest source of trouble.

She may have spoiled her only true human friendship, over an accusation that turned out to be bogus. Two weeks had passed, and she could feel the rift between her and Brandon growing wider and wider. If she didn't act now, she might never be able to heal what she had damaged so severely.

So, she decided to use Julie's advice. Brandon might not want to see her, or talk to her, but she was going to be assertive. She wasn't going to take no for an answer.

***

To her surprise, the door of the Watson house opened almost immediately upon her knocking. But the person who answered wasn't who she expected.

It was Brandon's mother Amy, sister of the late Jack Torres. Normally she was a happy woman, well put together, tidy to a fault... but today she looked disheveled. Her hair was lank and oily as though she hadn't showered in a number of days. She was wrapped in a blanket, and her eyes had the glassed over, dazed look of someone who hadn't stepped outside in a while.

"Jaz," she said, cracking a faint smile. "Nice to see you. You haven't been around in a long time."

"A couple of weeks," Jasmine said. She decided to come clean.

"Listen, Mrs. Watson... Brandon and I had a rough conversation and it was all my fault. I'd like to apologize to him and try to make things right, if he's here."

Amy nodded. "Let me check."

She receded into the house, pushing the door so that it was open only by a half inch. It wasn't an invitation to enter, but rather a promise that she would return. Jasmine heard the woman's footsteps fading into the house, then creaking up the stairs to the second floor. Obviously Amy knew whether or not her son was at home; she was just checking whether he actually wanted company.

After a minute or so Amy returned, opening the door with an apologetic smile and a shake of her head.

"I'm sorry, Jaz, but he's busy with something," she said. "But he did say he might come by the Nook later."

Jasmine nodded. "Thanks, Mrs. Watson."

She withdrew, casting a sad look back at the house as she and Luffy wandered down the sidewalk. Just when Brandon and his mother had truly gotten over the loss of his father, there had been another death in the family. It didn't seem fair. And, to Jasmine's distress, it almost seemed too unfair to be true.

But that was a concern for another time. She had a shift to get to.

***

Stepping into The Book Nook was like hugging a good friend you hadn't seen in a while. It had only been two days since her last shift, but she felt like it had been an eternity. As thrilling as the investigation into Jack's death was becoming, it still felt nice to sink into that old leather chair behind the counter and get lost in the world of books. It was a welcome respite in a town that was getting colder by the day, and not just due to the weather.

Of course, there was the matter of what she had learned about Patrick and Cynthia Jackson.

Her boss was his normal self as he shuffled around the store, cataloguing books and rearranging them. He was always on the lookout for what he called the perfect layout, an ideal floor plan and lineup of genre sections that would streamline the shopping process in the same way that was used in most grocery stores. He hadn't perfected it yet, and Jasmine doubted he would ever get it right in his own mind, but at least it gave Patrick something to do. Otherwise he might just stand in one spot tapping his foot nervously, wondering why no customers had come in during the past ten or fifteen minutes.

It was a slow shift. Glacial, really. The Nook stayed open all year round, but it relied on the tourism-heavy months to make the majority of its revenue per annum. These days, they were lucky to get a couple of locals in each hour, and even then they were usually the habitual shoppers who stopped in almost every day, just to check if there were any new books. They didn't usually buy much, because they had already scoured the store for everything that they could possibly want.

As such, Patrick was always anxious from about October to May. Constant worries plagued his mind. Whenever the lights flickered due to wind, he would glance up with terror, assuming the power company was cutting the cord on him.

If he had been calm, Jasmine might have asked her questions sooner. But instead she just sat at the counter doing busy work on the computer as her boss stomped around, walking endless laps and loops around the small store, always with a stack of books under his arm and a feverish glint in his eye.

Finally, somewhere close to two in the afternoon, all his nervous walking caught up to him and he got hungry. He brought his lunch up to the counter and ate beside Jasmine.

"Aren't you hungry?" he asked.

"I already had my lunch an hour and a half ago," she replied. "You know, at lunch time."

Patrick shrugged, ripping a bit of crust off his sandwich and dropping it for Luffy. The dog swallowed it before it hit the floor.

"Keep doing that and he might think he's your dog," said Jasmine.

"I should be so lucky. But at least I get to see him a few times a week. Right, boy?"

Luffy barked, licking his chops as he stared at Patrick's sandwich.

"Did you get all those new books entered in?" Patrick asked.

Jasmine nodded. "Yup. All twenty-six of them."

"Do you think this online database is really going to work? It'll automatically delete stuff when it sells?"

"That's what Brandon said, right?"

"That's what he told me. But he has a way of oversimplifying when he explains technology to me. I don't understand why. It's not like I'm an idiot."

Jasmine tried not to smile at that as she glanced over at the ancient monitor again. She was still amazed that Brandon had been able to install a fairly modern operating system on this old clunker.

She waited, trying not to let her own nerves show. She knew it was coming. Her chance. She just had to be patient and let Patrick get there on his own.

"So," he finally said when he was halfway through his sandwich and staring toward the door as if willing a huge gaggle of eager customers to come walking through. "How's your investigation going?"

"Good," she said. It was an understatement. "Actually, I think I had a major breakthrough yesterday. But there's something I wanted to ask you about, just out of curiosity."

"Okay," Patrick said, eager to make small talk.

"It's about Cynthia Jackson," Jasmine said, trying to sound casual, even somewhat disinterested, as she flipped through a random book in front of her.

"You want to talk about the most gorgeous woman in Blackwood Cove?" Patrick asked, laughing. "Go on down to the Leaky Trawler on the average night. Find the group of single guys who are just drunk enough to be sad. You'll hear all about her."

"I know enough about *her*," Jasmine said. "I've been training her dog, and we talk sometimes. But I was just curious about the two of you. And Jack."

Her disinterest was just an act. In reality, she was paying close attention. She was laser focused on Patrick, and she noticed when he suddenly went stiff.

"If you're talking about Jack's... *attitude* towards Cynthia and I, I don't have much to say," he replied. "The man saw an attack where there was none, and decided to attack me in return. I'm just glad he never harassed Cynthia the same way. I suppose he was too much in love to do that."

Jasmine nodded. "Were you and Cynthia ever...?"

"The two of us?" Patrick scoffed. "Goodness, no. Never. How could a worldly, beautiful person like Cynthia ever fall for a small-town, small business owner like myself? I had nothing to offer her."

"But that's not how love works," Jasmine said. "Didn't she ever have feelings for you? Or for Jack?"

"She liked the two of us just fine in middle school. We were friends, that was all. Sometimes we helped her with her homework, and sometimes she helped us with ours, depending on the subject. I think she was content to keep being friends forever, but Jack and I ruined that when we both independently decided to ask her to the school dance. It was her hint that we were after more than just friendship, but she didn't feel the same way about either of us. She tried to let us down easy. I got the hint, but Jack didn't. He was never very good at reading people. He wasn't very good at people in general."

"So, you and Cynthia stayed friends?" Jasmine asked.

Patrick nodded. "Yes. We were fairly close throughout high school. Then she got her big break into modeling, and she was off to see the world. When she had had enough of that, she went away to law school and figured out a way to live off the modeling work she had done for the rest of her life. Cynthia isn't just beautiful; she's brilliant as well. Probably the smartest person in the entire town. We'd all be better off if she was the mayor instead of that Eugene."

Jasmine almost asked about Eugene next, but she didn't want to let him push her off the current subject.

"So you don't think Jack ever bothered her?"

"Define bothered," Patrick said. "He never pulled any of the crap on her that he did with me, but that doesn't mean he left her alone. Jack was obsessed. Most people get over their first crush fairly quickly, but Jack never got over her. I suppose you can't blame him, but that doesn't excuse the way he used to follow her around."

"Used to?" Jasmine asked.

"When she finally came back to the Cove," Patrick explained. "For a while he was basically her shadow. He was stalking her. Back then, the police in the Cove were even slower to act than nowadays, so she wasn't able to do anything about it except complain to me. She said I was Jack's friend, and if anyone could talk some sense into him it was me."

"But you weren't friends anymore, were you?"

Patrick shook his head. "No, we were not. Long before Cynthia even left town, Jack had convinced himself that Cynthia and I had formed a secret tryst. A campaign against him, to make him feel spurned. I had nothing against Jack until he started acting like a fool. But still, I went to talk with him. I tried to explain that what he was doing was wrong, that he was making Cynthia feel unsafe and violating her privacy. I suppose my talk did work, though not in the way we planned. He mostly stopped bothering Cynthia, and started attacking me full time. He tried to convince the town that I was the real monster, that I was trying to keep Cynthia locked in a little bubble, acting as the lens through which she saw her own town and her own people..."

It sounded to Jasmine a lot like what Jack had been trying to say about Randy Ballard. Now that it seemed there was some truth to one smear campaign, she couldn't help but wonder about the other.

"You said he *mostly* stopped bothering her," Jasmine said.

"Well, he could never stay away for long. Eventually he would get jealous or sad, or lonely, and he would try and get involved in her life. He was very nearly successful. He caught Cynthia in a vulnerable time, right after her father passed away, and he was able to convince her into going on several dates with him until I intervened and talked some sense into her. After that, he turned his focus back to me and I don't think it ever left until he died. But you would have to ask Cynthia about that."

Patrick smiled. He was less tense now. He stood with an easy posture, as though saying all this had lifted a weight from his shoulders.

But was it a weight of guilt?

***

"Brandon!" Patrick called out. "What are you doing here? Come to help out an old man?"

"You're not that old," Brandon said quietly as he stepped through the vestibule and into the store. He looked nearly as manic as Patrick had earlier on. Something had gotten him quite excited; his cheeks were in full flush as he approached the counter.

"Brandon," Jasmine said, her mouth falling open as she struggled to think of the right words. "I just wanted to... I mean..."

"Don't worry about it," he said. "I can't stay very long, Jaz. But I just wanted to say you were wrong about me. I know who did it, and so will everyone else. Pretty soon."

"Brandon, I'm sorry about that," she said, wincing. Then the gravity of what he had said sunk in. "Wait, what do you mean? How do you know?"

"I've got eyes," he said, smirking clandestinely. "And ears. I'm not mad at you, Jaz. I'm not upset or anything. I just wanted you to know you don't have to worry about me."

There was so much she wanted to say but couldn't. Luckily, Brandon gave her a break. He immediately turned and walked out of the store, rendering further conversation impossible.

"What was that all about?" Luffy asked.

"I'm not sure," Jasmine said. "But even if he didn't kill Jack, he still has his secrets."

***

The Nook received a call from Sheriff Lustbader around 4:45.

He instructed Jasmine that she would not have to walk home tonight, but also that she ought to call her parents and inform them that she would be late. He gave no further information before hanging up.

As they locked up the Nook after closing, Jasmine noticed the plain grayish-silver sedan parked a little way up the street, the idle engine purring in the cold air.

"That's Ken's car, alright," Patrick said. "His off-duty car, I mean. Either he's taking you out for ice cream, or he's trying not to arouse the curiosity of the local populace."

He gave her a meaningful look, eyebrows raised. She smiled and shrugged her shoulders in return.

"Don't worry," she said. "You'll probably be hearing all about it pretty soon. But I'm not at liberty to spill any beans right now."

Luffy immediately put his nose to the sidewalk, sniffing around. "Someone spilled beans? Where?"

Patrick waved goodbye and started off toward home. After a moment's hesitation, Jasmine took a deep breath and went over to the parked car. She hadn't slept well last night. Her mind had been spinning uncontrollably since her time at the station yesterday, wondering feverishly what would happen next. And now that she was about to find out, her stomach kept flipping over.

The passenger window rolled down as she approached and Lustbader, dressed in civilian clothes and with his hair damp as though he'd just showered, gave her a wave.

"Hop on in," he said. "I just came from home. I had to get a nap in, I slept so terribly last night. Luffy can sit in the back."

"As opposed to the trunk?" the dog asked. "Thanks a lot, Sheriff. You're too kind."

Soon they were off, driving through town at a conservative fifteen miles an hour. Lustbader waited for entirely too long at each stop sign, looking both ways as though he expected someone to come running out in front of his car. He was a cautious man on a normal day, and today was far from normal.

"Dr. Reynolds phoned me half an hour ago," he said, finally

taking the last turn that would bring them up to the station. "He's got something for us."

"Did he tell you what?" Jasmine asked.

"Nope. Said he'd rather discuss it in person. I just hope it's good news. It would just be better for the whole town if Jack *did* die on accident, you know?"

"The truth has to come out no matter what," Jasmine reminded him.

"Of course. I know that. You can't blame a guy for trying. But I don't think it's looking good."

"Why not?"

"I had to bring Randy in and detain him this morning just to answer a few questions. On the advisement of Dr. Reynolds. I could have told Reynolds to forget it, but that would just give him more ammo against me."

"I guess the Doctor must have seen something he didn't like," Jasmine said.

"Or he's being cautious. Either way, the town's starting to notice that something's going on. I've already taken a dozen calls today about the Shoppe Right."

"What about it? Did they notice Randy wasn't there?"

"No, they noticed that the whole darn store is closed," Lustbader said. "And they're not happy about it."

Jasmine looked in the rearview mirror. Luffy met her gaze, and they stared at one another for a long moment.

Out of her six visions, two had already come true.

***

"Thank you all for coming here," Dr. Reynolds said, pacing along the edge of the conference table and running a finger along its shiny surface. He paused to take a swallow of coffee, carrying his cup with him as he continued pacing.

The rest of the department, as well as Jasmine and Luffy, sat on the opposite side of the table. No one said a word, but Jasmine glanced around and noticed that the three officers looked like coiled springs. Ready to jump up if someone so much as breathed on them. This was the most they had sweated in all their years of service. They watched the Doctor like a group of hawks. The lights were off in the room, and the scene was lit by the faint, shadowy light from an overhead projector.

"I have been working diligently for close to twenty-four hours with only short breaks for rest and sustenance," Dr. Reynolds went on. "My colleagues in the city have been working nearly as hard, acting to verify my findings. It can now be said with complete certainty that my conclusions are correct. We are not dealing with a very sophisticated criminal here. I mean no offense by this, but he is nothing but a small-town crook, and not a very impressive one."

"I knew Randy didn't have it in him to do all that dirty business," one of the other deputies said, a young fellow named Henry Bolen. "He never should have gotten mixed up in it."

"It's a shame," Lustbader agreed.

Dr. Reynolds stopped pacing again. A knowing smile crept slowly across his stoic features.

"I'm not talking about Mr. Ballard," he said. "I'm talking about Jack Torres."

The conference room filled with a chorus of squeaks and clanks as four people suddenly leaned forward on ancient office chairs.

"Excuse me, Dr. Reynolds," Lustbader said, "but what are you talking about?"

"I'm saying that the evidence is very clear to a trained eye," Dr. Reynolds replied. "The basic form used in the paperwork was legitimate. It was probably downloaded from a government website and printed out here in town. But beyond that, I'm afraid the deceit crumbles quickly. We have checked with your local accountant and verified that Mr. Ballard has been submitting similar paperwork each quarter for years and years. We asked to see the paperwork and the accountant provided us with the originals."

Here Dr. Reynolds grinned, looking around the room for a moment before he went on.

"Then," he said, "we compared the most recently filed

paperwork with that Miss... I mean *Deputy* Moore found under Jack's property."

Dr. Reynolds strolled to the overhead projector. He snapped a glove onto one hand and placed upon the projector a sheet of paper. Its image was cast upon the whiteboard.

"Here we have the top sheet from the pages from the bag Deputy Moore found," Dr. Reynolds continued. "If you look here, at the upper left corner, you will see a distinctive mark. Sort of a V with one short side. I spoke with one of my friends, a world-class expert, and he told me that this mark is a certain sign that we are looking at a copy. I didn't know what he meant until..."

He switched pages now, with one that looked very similar to the first.

"This sheet is taken from the most recent forms submitted by Mr. Ballard to his accountant. It's hard to tell by looking at what has been written on these forms. Or typed, rather. You see, in this day and age, a lot of paperwork is made up on a computer. Sometimes even the signature is electronic, an image that is pasted in. If everything is typed, it's very difficult to tell a copy from an original. In fact, there will be no difference between them at all. But if I direct your attention to the upper left corner again..."

Jasmine looked. The same exact mark was there, a V shape with one short side. Except it looked subtly different.

"This is ink," Dr. Reynolds said. "Not printer ink. The kind from a pen, actually. It was tested and confirmed. Someone, either the accountant or Mr. Ballard, accidently marked the page, probably while reading it with a pen tucked between their fingers. This is the very same mark found on the other sheet, except this one has actual pen ink involved. Which means it is the original, and the one found on Jack's property is a copy."

Dr. Reynolds turned back to his audience again, grinning now.

"The documents were heavily forged. Heavily and *clumsily*. Somehow Jack was able to procure these pages, scan them, and alter them on a computer. He did a fair job with falsifying the figures. Everything there was expertly done. He must have worked very hard on it. But in the end, it seems Randy Ballard is innocent."

The room was silent for a long time. Jasmine sat, frozen in disbelief. The investigation was not over after all. On the contrary, she had a strange feeling that it had only just begun.

"Do you think the accountant may have had anything to do with making the forgeries?" Lustbader asked.

"No," said Dr. Reynolds. "She would have had nothing to gain from it. In fact, I don't think even Mr. Ballard stood anything to gain from this. Why fill out an official document with figures that prove your own fraud? Now that we understand the truth, it all makes sense. Jack was desperate to discount Randy Ballard."

"But why?" Lustbader asked. "Why did he have it out for Randy so much? The two of them had no history at all."

"I suppose it was for the same reason Jack seemed to have it out for everyone around him," said Dr. Reynolds. "He was a lonely, spiteful man who couldn't fathom blaming himself for the troubles in his life. Perhaps he thought Randy was an easy target. I don't know. I'm not a psychologist. If we want to build a proper profile of Mr. Torres, we would need to get in contact with the FBI."

"Marsha Cargill would have a field day," Lustbader said with a sigh. "If she didn't have a heart attack first."

Suddenly, the Sheriff realized everyone was looking at him.

"Well," he said, "I guess we're back to square one. We thought Randy Ballard had a motive to kill Jack. We were wrong."

"So we're back to saying his death was an accident?" Jasmine asked.

"I'm afraid so."

She shook her head. "I'm not going to give up. I finally feel like I'm getting somewhere."

Lustbader stood up, prompting the other deputies to do the same. "I'm not asking you to give up, Jasmine. Keep on digging, if that's what you want to do. But as far as I'm concerned, Jack Torres was a mean son of a gun who got himself into trouble and was too drunk to get out of it. He tried to shut down a good man, a sound businessperson. I won't say 'good riddance,' but..."

He nodded once to Dr. Reynolds and made his way out of the conference room.

CHAPTER 10

When Jasmine wasn't working, she wandered aimlessly. Sometimes she prayed for another vision to come, but her prayers were not answered. There were things still left to look into, items that she hadn't yet checked off on her to-do list. But she couldn't summon the strength or the concentration to tend to any of them.

For the second time during her investigation, she felt lost. Adrift in a sea of conflicting information.

Adrift in a sea...

She was somewhere on Bristol Lane when her phone rang. It was Julie Barnes. It wasn't the first call the editor had made to her recently, but this time Jasmine decided to answer it.

"Where have you been?" Julie asked. "I thought you would have been back by now."

She didn't sound angry. A little concerned, maybe.

"Sorry," said Jasmine. "I just don't know where to go next. I'm lost."

"Well, that makes two of us. A bit crazy about Randy, isn't it? Strike number one thousand against Jack Torres. It seems like every person in town had a reason to want him dead, but no one did it. They're all too damn honest and nice."

"We'll see," Jasmine replied.

"Still think it was murder? That's the spirit. I'm glad to hear it, Jasmine. I was starting to think I was alone again."

"You're not," Jasmine promised. "I'm just trying to figure out what to do next. Have you had any luck talking to the Carters?"

"Not at all. How about you?"

"I haven't even tried."

"Then we'll just have to hope neither one of them is a legitimate suspect. Listen, I know there probably isn't anything new to talk about..."

There was, but Jasmine said nothing.

"...but I'd like to get together again," Julie finished. "Just so we can brainstorm a bit. Do you think you could swing by the Herald office again?"

"Yeah, sure. I can be there in fifteen minutes."

"Great! I'll see you then. You may have to wait a little bit, though. I have a meeting with a gentleman from out of town."

They ended the call and Jasmine turned around on Bristol, heading back up through town. Five minutes later, as she was winding her way through side streets, she heard a police siren in the distance. The car came racing through town and passed by her a few blocks over, going fast. It was followed closely by a second car.

"What do you think that was about?" Luffy asked when the sound had faded a bit.

"Dunno," Jasmine said. "Maybe someone else drowned mysteriously."

She pulled out her phone and dialed Sheriff Lustbader. Both his office and his mobile phone. There was no answer on either. Jasmine stood in the street, tapping her foot and chewing her lip. In the end, she decided to make good on her promise to Julie. If the police were on to something that concerned her, she knew Lustbader would return her call eventually.

Main Street was as deserted as ever on a cold late-autumn day. The sky was gray, letting through an occasional sliver of sun that highlighted rather than alleviated the morose feeling that hung over the Cove. Thankfully, the Herald's office building was warm and bright. There was an aroma of fresh coffee in the air, and classical music was playing from a small radio on the secretary's desk.

"Jasmine Moore?" the woman asked, glancing up from her tiny, square computer screen.

Jasmine nodded.

"Julie will be with you shortly. Feel free to have a seat."

Jasmine and Luffy moved into the tiny waiting area. There were three chairs, a low table littered with old copies of the Cove Herald, a stack of wax-lined paper cups, and a carafe of complimentary coffee. Jasmine got herself a cup and glanced through a few of the papers. They depicted better times. Safer times. More mundane times. The cover story on one issue was of a record-breaking pumpkin that someone had grown.

Did Jasmine miss those times? The times when the most exciting thing that happened was the arrival of a new book at the Nook, or a new batch of them at the Blackwood Cove Library?

That was a good question, one she had been asking herself for some time. She was on the verge of answering it definitively, but part of her felt guilt and shame about what the answer would be.

She was still staring at the same black and white image of a huge pumpkin when she heard a door open in the distance. She looked up and saw Marlon Gale stepping back into the lobby. Today he was dressed in a suit, stiffly starched and perfectly tailored. It was a rare sight in the Cove.

Marlon gave her a nod and turned, preparing to leave the building.

But Jasmine wasn't about to let him go. She set her coffee down and hopped out of the chair, rushing to cut him off.

"Oh, are you leaving too?" Marlon asked. "After you, then. I'll get the door."

Jasmine smiled. "Enjoying your tour of our humble little town, Mr. Gale?"

He gave her an appraising look, then an innocent smile. "Yes, I am. It's a nice little place. A far cry from the chaos of the city."

"You're not fooling anybody," Jasmine replied. "At least, you're not fooling *me*. What kind of tourist comes this late in the year? And who even wears a suit like that?"

Self-consciously, he reached up to adjust one of his lapels. "I understand I must stick out like a sore thumb around here. But where I come from, it's customary to dress nicely when meeting with important people."

"Julie Barnes, huh? What were you two talking about?"

Marlon smiled, attempting to push past her. She stepped with him, continuing to bar his way.

"If you really have to know," he relented, "I was curious about the history of this place. I've already been to the library and read everything I could, but nothing beats hearing it from the mouth of a local. And I figured the editor of the Herald would be able to provide the best possible account."

"I'm sure that's half right," Jasmine replied.

She finally stepped aside. Marlon stepped past her and out into the cold; Jasmine followed close behind. He glanced over his shoulder, saw her there, and sighed.

"It's the entire truth, actually," he said.

"No it isn't. I saw you outside Jack Torres's cottage the other day. After we ran into each other. What are you here for, Mr. Gale?"

He waved over his shoulder to her, then ducked into the nearby bakery. As the door opened, the smell of cinnamon rolls wafted out, which gave Jasmine a second reason to follow Marlon inside. But she knew instinctively that she wouldn't figure anything out by asking *him*. He wasn't going to budge.

So she returned to the Herald office, and the secretary waved her through.

When Jasmine entered the office at the end of the hall, she found Julie relaxing with her feet up on the desk.

"Good to see you," the editor said, dragging her feet down and fixing a messy stack of papers. "Sit down, if you'd like."

"I don't think I'll be here long," Jasmine said decisively.

"Oh? Do you have another appointment somewhere?"

"Something tells me I will," Jasmine replied, thinking of the police sirens. "And something tells me you might not want me to stick around for long after my next few questions. Why were you talking with that Gale guy?"

Julie sat forward, folding her hands on her desk. "Marlon? He's a lovely gentleman who arrived in town recently. He was curious about our history, that's all. And by the way, what makes you think you can come into my office and start demanding information?"

"You told me to be assertive," Jasmine replied. "You can't have me both ways, Julie."

The editor shrugged. "I guess not. I'll have to be more careful with my advice from now on. Young people have a way of turning everything around on you. But I didn't figure you for the rebellious type, Jasmine."

"Are you disappointed?"

"No. On the contrary, I'm impressed. I see the same qualities in you that I possessed when I was your age. The old Herald staff kept on being annoyed by my prying, right up until they started having to report to me."

"Well, I'm not going to take your job," Jasmine said. "I'm just sick of trying to puzzle everything out on my own. I need answers, and you're going to give them to me."

Julie scoffed. "Answers? What makes you think I have any? I'm in the same boat as you. We're both trying to figure out for certain what happened to Jack, and neither of us has made much progress."

"That's true. But there is one thing you can tell me. Were you and Jack Torres ever involved with each other?"

This question seemed to hit Julie like a slap in the face. She reared back in her chair and sat in stunned silence for a moment.

"No one has brought that up to me for twenty years," she finally said. "I had thought it was forgotten history. Who told you about it? Was it Patrick?"

"Why would Patrick tell me?" Jasmine asked.

"Because he was the one who set us up! After Cynthia moved away, he approached me almost immediately. His goal was to make Jack forget his foolish crush, and it worked for a while. I liked Patrick, as a friend, so I went along with his plan. I never thought that I..."

"You never thought you would actually fall for Jack," Jasmine said.

Julie let out a sigh that almost sounded like a cry of despair. She stood up and went to a filing cabinet in the corner of the room. Brushing aside a few hanging leaves, she unlocked the top drawer and began fishing around in the very back. After a moment she pulled something out and stared down at it reverently.

Julie's back was to her. Jasmine couldn't see much. She and Luffy sidestepped, craning their necks, and were able to make out the faded edge of an old photograph.

"Kind of a self-fulfilling prophecy, huh?" Luffy said. "This is a bit creepy, Jasmine."

Julie turned around and lay the photo on the desk carefully. It was the very same one Jasmine had seen in her vision. Jack and Julie were both quite recognizable, now that she was seeing the photo head on.

"I was in love," Julie said. "Jack blossomed with me. He grew confident. He started to speak out and actually be heard. He was a completely different person while we were together."

"How long did it last?" Jasmine asked.

"A few years. I was a young fool, and I thought Jack felt the same way about me as I did about him. But it just wasn't the case. The whole time, he was still thinking of Cynthia. I was his way of striking back at her, of perhaps showing her what she was missing out on. In his twisted mind, he probably thought she would come running to him as soon as she got home. I had my first inkling of this when I found a letter he had written to her but hadn't posted yet. The letter spoke of how wonderful his life was, how everything was just perfect and how he wished one day she might find something similar. He even included a photo of us together... The very same photo you're looking at now. I intercepted that letter, but I'm sure he sent out dozens."

"I'm sorry, Julie," Jasmine said.

"I'm sure you are. You're a good kid, Jasmine, which is why I'm answering your questions at all. Now I'm starting to realize something... perhaps I'm too deeply involved in this. I'm trying to avenge the man I loved, to prove to this whole town that he wasn't just a crazy old hermit who hated everyone. He might not have loved me while we were together, but he treated me well. He was a gentle person, deep down."

Julie stowed the picture again, treating it like a fragile relic as she slid it back into the file cabinet.

"The thing is," she added as she slid the drawer shut, "he may not need avenging at all. Some part of me refuses to believe Jack died of his own foolishness... but of course, that's probably just what happened, isn't it? People change. I knew him as a tender and caring young man with a wounded heart. But that's not who he was when he died."

Jasmine walked around the desk. At first she thought she would only pat the other woman on the arm, but suddenly she found herself embracing Julie, pulling her into a tight hug that lasted for several moments.

"I'm not going to stop, and neither should you," Jasmine said.

But Julie shook her head. "Go on. This is your story. I'll help you write it, but that's where my involvement ends now."

Jasmine nodded. As much as she wanted the help, she had to respect Julie's decision.

"I'll keep you updated," she said.

"You'd better," Julie replied. "Now get out there and get back to work."

***

Lustbader still hadn't called. Jasmine was growing increasingly antsy the longer she waited, but she didn't want to spoil the good will she had managed to build up by butting in one too many times.

"Patience is a virtue," she told Luffy, scratching his ears. "Let's go see Brandon."

"Why?" Luffy asked.

"Because I have some things I need to say to him."

***

This time, the door to the Watson house did not open for a

long time.

At last, after Jasmine rang the bell a third time, she heard footsteps booming down the hall. The door flew open and Brandon Watson stared out, looking agitated. He had a video game controller in one hand and a headset covering his ears.

"Oh, Jasmine!" he said, fumbling as he tried to remove the headset and dropping it to the floor.

Jasmine scooped it up as she stepped inside, not waiting for an invitation. She held onto the headset, refusing to give it back until Brandon heard her out. From the earpieces, she heard the faint hiss of video game sounds.

"Pretty good range on this thing," she remarked.

"It's Bluetooth," Brandon said. "Patrick's never heard of it, but I'm sure you have."

She shrugged, moving past him down the hall. He stared after her for a moment, perhaps in shock at her newfound audacity, then rushed to follow her.

Jasmine entered the kitchen. She shoved one side of the headset into her pocket, then grabbed a glass from the cupboard and filled it with water. After taking a sip, she noticed Luffy staring up at her with eager eyes.

"Do you have a bowl I can use?" Jasmine asked, gesturing to the dog.

"Oh!" Brandon moved into action, setting his controller down and reaching into a lower cupboard. He came out with a shallow metal mixing bowl and filled it for Luffy. As the dog lapped away at the water, Brandon stared around the room awkwardly.

"I just had a conversation with somebody," Jasmine said. "And I realized something. I don't want either of us to grow up into something we aren't. You know?"

"Like my uncle?" Brandon asked.

She nodded. "Everyone in town seems to have at least one good memory of him. Either they used to be friends, or lovers, or something... but then again, everyone in town also hated him. Hardly anyone cared when he died. I just think that's really sad. Somewhere along the way it all went sour."

Brandon shrugged. "It was his own fault. The guy was a complete jerk."

"I'm not saying it wasn't his fault. I'm just saying I don't want either of us to grow up resentful, or full of regrets, or... whatever. I just want us to be who we are now. A little older, a little wiser, but essentially the same people."

"Okay," Brandon said uncertainly.

"That 'date' we went on was a big mistake," Jasmine went on. "And I don't mean just because of my stupid questions. I never should have gotten your hopes up. I like you, Brandon, but not the same way you like me. No more hoping for something that will never happen, okay? I don't want to be the thing you never let go of, the reason you turn mean."

"I'm not going to turn mean," Brandon said. "I pretty much already knew you didn't want to be my girlfriend, Jasmine, but I guess... well, you know."

"Yeah, I know."

They looked at each other, then they looked at Luffy, and then they started laughing. At first the laughter was nervous and shaky, but soon it became something else. It was catharsis.

"So," Brandon said. "Do you still think I might have killed my uncle?"

Jasmine shook her head. "Nah. You could never do that."

"Dang. I was hoping you'd say yes, so I could rub it in your face. I have proof, Jasmine."

He beckoned to her, and the three of them went upstairs and into Brandon's room. Jasmine was always surprised by how tidy this space was. She usually expected an unmade bed, bags of snacks scattered around, dirty laundry on the floor. But it was as neat as an army bunkhouse.

Jasmine sat on the bed and watched as Brandon went to his desk and started picking through a pile of papers in the corner. He came back with a tiny rectangular object. It was a business card, or something close to it.

"Read it," Brandon said, handing the card over.

"Marlon Gale," Jasmine read aloud, "Federal Bureau of

Investigations. Oh, crap! All this time I thought he had something to do with Jack's death. But now you're telling me he's with the FBI? Are you kidding?"

Brandon shook his head as he sat next to her. "My mom knows Marlon's uncle from college. They were pretty good friends. We like Sheriff Lustbader a lot, but we didn't think he really had what it takes to figure out what happened to Uncle Jack."

"So you called in a federal agent," Jasmine said. "When you already knew I was on the job. Thanks for the vote of confidence."

Brandon shrugged. "I'm sure if you went through all the intensive training that FBI people have to go through, you'd be better at the job than him."

"How flattering. So what's the deal? Does this guy report back to you?"

"He keeps us updated on the progress of his investigation. But I don't think he tells us everything. I'm sure the real truth is in whatever reports he sends back to headquarters."

"Then we have no idea what he's getting up to," said Jasmine. "Because he sure hasn't been working with our police department."

"How do you know that?"

"Because *I've* been working with them. I've never seen Marlon around, and no one at the station has ever mentioned him."

"Really? You've been back in the station? I thought that note Lustbader gave you was just for a laugh."

"It was, at first. Then I proved I was worth a little more than that."

Brandon nodded. "Nice going. But how did you prove it?"

"Did you know Randy Ballard was brought in to the station?"

"Yeah, I heard. The Shoppe Right was closed too."

"Well, I can't say much yet. Not until Lustbader decides to make the information public. But let's just say I found some evidence that painted Randy as a suspect. He was absolved, but the fact remains I did something the police weren't able to do."

"Like dig up a bag of falsified documents under the sand by

Uncle Jack's house?"

Jasmine stared. "How did you...?"

"Agent Gale. He told us about it."

"Then how did he...?"

Brandon shrugged.

"Unless..." Jasmine narrowed her eyes. "Oh, the sneaky son of a... He's been hacking into our information. Instead of getting it from Lustbader, he must be getting it from HQ. They're probably tapped into the flow of data from every single police department in the country, even the small ones."

"I'm sure they are," said Brandon. "They wouldn't be very effective if they weren't."

"I guess Marsha Cargill was right again. I hate when that happens. So Marlon knows everything that I know, along with everything the police know... and maybe some other things that no one else knows but him and his boss. Brandon, there's no way I'm going to let some out of town fed steal my investigation. I need to talk to him. Do you know where he's staying?"

"At the only hotel in the Cove," Brandon said. "Where else? It's not like he's been sleeping on our couch. Even though my mom might like it if he did. I swear she has a crush on him."

"Well," Luffy chimed in, "she has been single for a long time."

And, Jasmine thought, Marlon's interest in Blackwood Cove and all its denizens would evaporate as soon as this case was closed. Hopefully Amy Watson wouldn't get too attached.

"I have one more thing to ask you," Jasmine said. "Do you want to come with me, or would you rather sit this out?"

Brandon thought about it for a long moment. Then he smiled, reaching out to take her hand.

CHAPTER 11

Located even further out than the Shoppe Right, on the very fringe of town, the Cozy Cove Lodge was your standard hotel with a facade that made it seem to be constructed of logs. It looked rustic from the road, and outdated from up close.

The hotel office was a dusty place full of stale smells. Which was not to say it was dirty. There were no stains on the floor, walls, or ceiling. No garbage scattered around. It just looked like a crypt that had been recently opened. And if it looked like a crypt, then the clerk resembled whatever desiccated corpse had been found within it.

Lee Aubrey was a man who had seen the Cove in every one of its eras. He had been born when the town was just a smattering of log houses built to accommodate the fishermen and their families. Once the cannery moved in, and the fishing operations were taken over by a larger entity, Lee's father had decided to go into the hotel business. And Lee had been here ever since.

"Greetings, travelers," the ancient man rattled out as he shuffled up to the counter. "What can I do for you? A room? Say, I think you may be too young to be sharing a room alone. But my eyes aren't what they used to be..."

"We're both nineteen," Jasmine said quickly, giving Brandon an awkward look. "But we're not here to rent a room. We need to talk to one of your guests. Marlon Gale."

"Who's that?" Lee asked, cocking his ear toward her.

"Marlon Gale!" Jasmine said louder. "He's a tall guy. Friendly and kind of private."

"I'll take a look at my ledger," Lee said, using a claw-like hand to drag over a huge logbook. He turned to the last filled out page and started scanning through items.

"He's a black guy," Brandon said. "And he's with the FBI."

Lee slammed the book shut. "Why didn't you just say that? He's in room five. But don't tell him I ratted him out. I don't want J. Edgar Hoover to come raiding my hotel, you know."

Jasmine couldn't tell if it was a joke or a sign of dementia.

They left the old man to his devices and stepped outside. It wasn't hard to find room five, and a moment later they were knocking at its door.

"I hope he's here and not out searching for clues," Brandon said.

But his fears were settled when the shades on the window shifted to the side. Jasmine caught a brief glimpse of someone staring out at her before the shades fell back in place again. There was a clicking sound and the door opened, stopping short due to the chain lock. A single dark eye peered out.

"I didn't order any room service," Marlon joked in a guarded tone. "I think you two must have the wrong room."

"Doesn't he mean we *three*?" Luffy complained.

"She knows, Agent Gale," Brandon said. "I told her that my mom and I called you in. She knows you're trying to solve the same crime that she is."

"Who said there's been a crime?" Marlon asked. "I don't even know what you're talking about."

"Jack Torres!" Brandon said. "My uncle."

"Last I heard," Marlon replied, "it wasn't a crime to get drunk and drown yourself."

"Cut the crap," Jasmine said. "And open the door."

Marlon chuckled. "No, I don't think I will do that, thank you very much. Have a nice day."

The door shut. Brandon sighed, shaking his head. But Jasmine wasn't ready to give up. She hammered at the door with her fist incessantly for almost a minute, until Marlon had had enough.

"Go away!" he shouted from inside the room.

"No!" Jasmine shouted back. "If you don't let us in, I'll tell Sheriff Lustbader and the mayor that there's an FBI agent sniffing around!"

The door opened again, but still only by a tiny crack. The chain lock was still in place.

"So what?" Marlon asked. "My authority supersedes that of the local government and law enforcement."

"But I know for a fact Eugene Carter won't be so happy that you didn't even have the courtesy to warn him you'd be in his town," Jasmine said. "You'll save yourself a big headache if you just let me in. We need to talk."

"About what?" Marlon asked.

"About everything. We can help each other out. I'm not stupid, and I'm not going to leave you alone until-"

He interrupted her by slamming the door. But she heard him disengaging the chain. He opened the door again, stepping aside to let them through. He was dressed down again, in a gray t-shirt and a pair of sweat pants.

"Come right on in," he said, in a tone that was only slightly annoyed.

Jasmine went through first, peering around. Marlon hadn't done much to customize his room. There were a few changes of clothes in the closet. His badge was sitting on the TV stand, but his gun was nowhere to be seen. He probably kept it hidden.

"Nice place," Jasmine said.

"It's definitely a lot nicer than the office," Marlon said, closing the door as the others came inside. "I was pleasantly surprised. But you didn't come here to chat about interior design, and frankly I don't want any more of my time to be wasted than necessary."

"You're a lot snippier than the last few times we met," Jasmine remarked.

"That was because I didn't know you would soon be a pain in... well, let's not go there."

"Besides, it didn't seem like you were very busy when we got here," Brandon said, trying to play peacemaker.

"I don't have to explain my procedures to either of you," said Marlon. He walked calmly to the bed and sat down, turning on the TV but lowering the volume so it was barely audible.

"Why are you here, Agent Gale?" Jasmine asked.

He replied without looking away from the news. "I had nothing else going on, and a family friend thought they needed my help. My boss okayed the assignment and here I am."

"Do you believe Jack Torres was murdered?"

"It doesn't matter what I believe. My opinions are of no consequence."

"Of course they are. You're not a robot. No matter how professional you try to be, your own feelings and thoughts will always intrude."

"Well, you're right about that," Marlon admitted. "Now I'm going to ask you something, Ms. Moore. What do you think you're doing?"

"I'm figuring things out. And it seems to me like I'm ahead of you, Agent."

"Because you dug up a bag of phony crap?" Marlon shook his head. "I was hoping that would lead to something too, but it didn't. You're at square one. Don't try and deny it."

Jasmine folded her arms. "Which square are you on, then?"

"At least two or three," he replied with a smile. "I'm the one who's ahead, Jasmine. Just a little while ago your Sheriff and his deputies responded to a call from a man named Donald Parks. Right now they're probably scratching their heads, trying to figure out exactly what to do. In five minutes or less your phone will ring, and it will be Sheriff Lustbader."

"How do you know all that?" Brandon asked in awe.

He extended one arm, palm up. Then he took the fingers of his other hand and pressed them to his wrist. "I have a finger on the pulse. This is my job. I can't always predict the future, but I can get a reasonable approximation."

"That sounds familiar," Luffy said, glancing meaningfully up at Jasmine.

"Right now," Marlon went on, "my heart rate is at about fifty-five beats per minute. I'm calm. Nothing is currently bothering me. Do you know why?"

Jasmine shook her head.

"Because Jack Torres probably wasn't murdered," Marlon said. "And even if he was, it was a crime of passion. Something done in a heavy moment. Unplanned. We're not dealing with a serial killer here. We're just dealing with a normal person whose emotions got out of hand. There won't be a second murder in this town. I'm not even convinced there's been *one*."

"Then what kind of call were the cops responding to?" Brandon asked.

Marlon didn't answer. Instead, he looked at Jasmine and smiled, giving her an encouraging nod. *Go ahead.*

"I think Donald must have found something," Jasmine said, narrowing her eyes as she thought hard. "A piece of evidence."

"Something very obvious," Marlon added. "I met this Donald Parks guy. Talked to him. He has cataracts in both eyes. If it was anything that was easy to miss, he never would have seen it."

"Then *what?*" Brandon asked impatiently.

"Something that wasn't there at first," Jasmine said, struggling to breathe, "but has suddenly appeared."

Marlon nodded.

"I don't understand," Brandon said.

Jasmine was about to answer, but her phone rang. The electronic chime filled the room, startling everyone but Agent Gale. Even Luffy jumped, staring at Jasmine's pocket as though it contained an angry cobra.

She took the phone out and answered the call. She put it on speaker phone so the room could hear.

"Sheriff?" she said.

"Deputy Moore," Lustbader replied. His voice contained a hint of the usual good humor, but it was buried beneath a layer of unease. "I don't know if you've heard yet, but we've got something. If you want to take part, join us on the beach by

Jack's place as soon as possible."

He hung up. Jasmine looked around the room. First at Brandon, then at Agent Gale, and finally at Luffy. In unison, without speaking a single word, they all began to move. Marlon grabbed his handgun from the drawer of the bedside table, then scooped up his badge on his way out of the door.

**

They all jammed into Marlon Gale's cramped car and headed for the beach. Marlon parked against the curb on Bristol Lane and they jogged down a ways until they came to the sandy path that led down to the cottages. Outside the first one, they found Donald Parks watering a few plants. He turned to give them a half-hearted wave, then went back to his work.

Jack's cottage was deserted. There was no one around it. But they didn't have to look far to see where the hubbub was; Sheriff Lustbader, his two deputies, and Dr. Reynolds were all gathered near the water in rubber boots. There was a camera involved, and a notebook in which one deputy was scrawling furious notes, as dictated by an animated Dr. Reynolds.

The object of their scrutiny was plain. A small fishing boat was sitting there on the beach. It listed to one side, ready to tip over. Beneath it, the sand was plowed up in a deep furrow. Large waves continued pushing against the boat, shoving it up the beach in tiny increments, causing it to wobble briefly from side to side each time.

"That's Uncle Jack's boat!" Brandon said.

He started to run, but Marlon caught his arm.

"Easy," the agent advised. "Let's walk."

They moved toward the water at a casual pace. When they were twenty feet away, Lustbader finally turned and spotted them. At first he looked at Jasmine and smiled a little. Then, when he saw who was accompanying her, his smile became a confused frown.

"Brandon, I think you should be home with your mother right now," said the Sheriff.

"He's working with me," Jasmine said.

Lustbader sighed. "Of course he is. And who's this guy?"

Marlon immediately whipped out his badge and held it out. "Agent Marlon Gale, FBI."

Lustbader glanced at the badge, then at the man. Then he looked at the badge again, for much longer this time. He shook his head, looking quite shocked.

"I'm sorry, Agent Gale, but we don't require your services on this case," said Lustbader. "So far it's been a very simple investigation. Routine."

Marlon smiled. "Then why did your squad cars come screaming down here at sixty miles an hour with their sirens on?"

"Because," Dr. Reynolds said, joining them, "we didn't want the boat disturbed by the local ruffians before we were able to get a good look at it. As an FBI agent, I'm sure you understand the importance of maintaining the sanctity of all evidence. By the way, I'm Dr. Raymond Reynolds."

Lustbader turned, staring at the Doctor. "Was this your idea, Reynolds? Did you call this guy in?"

Dr. Reynolds shook his head. "Not at all. In fact, I had no idea the FBI was involved."

"The Bureau *isn't* involved," Marlon said, stowing his badge. "It's just me. This is something of a personal matter. Amy Watson, formerly Amy Torres, is a good friend of my uncle's. I'm here undertaking my own personal investigation. My boss okayed the time away, but that's all."

Dr. Reynolds nodded. "Then with all due respect, Agent Gale, you don't have the authority to interfere with this scene."

"Not yet, but I can get it," Marlon replied. "The more I look into this case, Doctor, the more I see a cause for FBI involvement. With all due respect to you in return, and to you, Sheriff, I think you could use a bit of help."

Dr. Reynolds turned red with barely concealed anger.

Sheriff Lustbader nodded. "Maybe we could."

"It would take time to gain full approval from my superiors to take over," said Marlon. "But we could get around that process with your agreement. I won't do anything until you give me the go-ahead, Sheriff."

"Okay," said Lustbader. "Consider the go-ahead given. I'm glad to have you here, Agent."

They shook hands.

Dr. Reynolds stared at them for a moment, then shucked his gloves and shoved them into his pocket. "Then I suppose you no longer require my services. I'll be at the hotel if you should need me."

He went stomping up the beach, back onto Bristol Lane.

"Dr. Reynolds is a brilliant man," Lustbader said. "I hope you know what you're doing, Agent Gale."

Marlon smiled, turning his attention to the fishing boat. "We can call him back later, if it comes to that. Tell me what you know."

Lustbader led the way as they walked slowly toward the boat. "It ran aground sometime in the past couple of hours. No one saw it until just a little while ago. A man named Donald Parks spotted it, and recognized it as belonging to Jack Torres."

"Have you been aboard yet?" Marlon asked.

Lustbader shook his head. "No. We were trying to be as cautious as possible. Dr. Reynolds gave it a thorough search with his eyes and didn't come up with much. We were getting ready to climb up when you arrived."

They stopped a few feet before the boat. On land, without any of its hull hidden beneath the water, it towered over them. Marlon stared up at the sharp bow ridge, rubbing his chin.

"She doesn't look very stable," he said. "Not many of us will be able to walk around on deck at a time. I'd like to get up there first, if you don't mind."

"Go right ahead," said Lustbader.

Marlon looked around, sizing everyone up. "Unfortunately, I'm on the heavy side. So I'll need someone light. How much do you weigh, Sheriff?"

"I dunno, about one-seventy."

"And you, deputies?"

They just shrugged their shoulders.

"Jasmine?" Marlon asked, turning to her with a smile that said he had everything worked out.

"One-nineteen last time I checked," she replied.

"And I'm only seventy!" Luffy shouted. "Pick me!"

"Jasmine and I will go in and see what we can find," Marlon said.

One of the deputies offered the huge camera he was holding, but Marlon shook his head and pulled out his phone.

As he and Jasmine skirted the edge of the boat, searching for a good way up, Luffy was hot on their heels. He was prancing in the sand, wagging his tail, whining when they wouldn't pay attention to him.

"Don't leave me behind," he said. "I promise I'll be light! I won't tip the boat over, I swear..."

"This should work," Marlon said. They had come to the side where the ship had sagged into the sand, lowering the height of the deck railing. Marlon crouched down, offering his hands as a boosting platform.

Jasmine gave Luffy a few pets before she sprang up, launching from Marlon's hands and hauling herself over onto the deck of the boat.

"Jasmine, wait!" Luffy cried in anguish.

"You too, Luffy," Marlon said. "As long as you promise to behave."

A moment later the dog was frantically clawing his way over the railing as well. As soon as he landed on the other side he ran to Jasmine. Marlon followed him over soon after, expertly vaulting over the railing and landing lightly on his feet. He must have weighed close to two hundred pounds, but the boat didn't shift at all.

"Okay," he said. "First things first. Don't touch anything except with your eyes. Tread lightly. Watch where you put your feet. That means you too, Luffy."

"He'll behave," Jasmine promised.

And so he did, following behind and walking where they

walked as they strode across the deck, their eyes taking in everything.

"I feel like things are missing," Marlon said. "I don't see a life preserver, for one. It must have fallen off the deck in rough seas, with no one onboard to steer the boat properly. I just hope we're not missing anything crucial."

Their search was as thorough as it could be without touching anything. But the boat was quite small, and it wasn't long before they reached the cabin at the bow end. The door was latched shut; Marlon used his clothed elbows to open it.

But the door only opened by a fraction. Something was blocking it.

"Damn," Marlon said. "I can't even get my arm through that."

"Just shove it," Jasmine suggested.

Marlon shook his head. "I don't know what's blocking it. It could be important. I don't want to disturb the scene any more than necessary."

"Then let me try," Jasmine said.

He stepped aside. Jasmine approached the crack in the door and tried to fold her body into it. She managed to get her arm through, but it was plain that not all of her was going to fit.

"Here, take my phone," Marlon said.

Jasmine pulled her arm back out to take it. He had it set to record video. The flash was on, so they would be able to see inside the dark cabin.

Jasmine stuck her arm through again, and turned the phone slowly and carefully in as smooth an arc as she could manage. She then withdrew, and they huddled together to view the video.

It turned out the blockage was nothing more than an upended trunk. It was heavy, constructed of metal, but the lid was open and they could see what was inside. A couple of life vests, a battery powered lantern, some emergency rations, flares, and a pack of bottled water. Not much else.

But as the video continued, Marlon spotted something and paused it, giving them a freeze frame.

"There!" he said, pointing at a tiny section of the screen.

Jasmine narrowed her eyes, trying to figure out what it was he was pointing at. It was something small, rectangular, greenish-white in color...

"It's money," she said. "So what?"

"That's a one-hundred-dollar bill, Jasmine," Marlon replied. "I can tell. I've studied these things."

At first it didn't seem like a big deal to Jasmine. But the more she thought about it, the more her original logic began to fall apart.

"What kind of fisherman goes out to sea with cash?" she asked.

Marlon. "Right. Let alone a one-hundred-dollar bill. It's not like there's a whole lot to buy on the open sea, unless the Shoppe Right has a marine branch. But let's give Jack the benefit of the doubt. Maybe he kept some cash on him in case of a rainy day. Or in case he had to swim fifteen miles down the coast again and washed up in a strange town. Or maybe he just forgot he had a bill in his pocket when he got onboard that night."

Marlon hit play on the video. But he almost immediately paused it again, pointing at something else.

"What is it?" Luffy asked.

"A briefcase," Jasmine replied. "Open. And empty."

"To ask a similar question," Marlon said, "what kind of fisherman goes out to sea with a briefcase? Especially a nice one like that."

Jasmine remembered something. "Ruby! My neighbor. She told me that on her last visit to Jack's cottage she thought she saw some cash hidden under a jacket on his couch. A *lot* of cash."

"And now we have a hundred-dollar bill," Marlon said, "along with a briefcase that could easily have been used to carry more. My guess is, someone was in a hurry to get all the cash out of it, and they ended up dropping one of the bills on the floor."

"Why wouldn't they just take the briefcase?" Luffy wondered.

Jasmine reiterated his question for Marlon.

"I don't know," Marlon replied. "Maybe the briefcase was too recognizable. It could have Jack's monogram on it. It would have been too conspicuous to carry around."

"So someone killed him for his money?" Jasmine asked.

"I don't know that either. But whatever the case is, money *was* involved in some way."

They watched the rest of the video. When it reached its end, Marlon clicked his tongue in disappointment.

"We might find something else here with a more thorough search," he said. "But my time is running out, Jasmine."

"What do you mean?" she asked.

"My daughter's birthday is the day after tomorrow," he said with a smile. "I haven't missed it yet, and I don't plan on it this year."

Jasmine grabbed the sleeve of his jacket. "You can't leave now! We're just getting somewhere."

"Maybe we are, maybe we aren't," he said. "You can never tell. Some cases start off remarkably strong, then peter out. Next thing you know, thirty years go by and they're sitting deep in a filing cabinet somewhere, gathering dust and as cold as can be."

"This isn't going to be like that!" said Jasmine. "Will you at least come back? Please?"

He shrugged. "It might not be me. But I'll make sure you have help from someone."

She shook her head, staring at the deck beneath her feet.

"Chin up," Marlon said. "You've got me for today and tomorrow. Let's make the most of it."

***

"What do you make of this?" Marlon asked.

They were back on the beach, playing the video again. Sheriff Lustbader leaned in, staring at the freeze frame image of the open briefcase.

"That's my dad's!" Brandon suddenly cried out.

Everyone turned to look at him.

"He was a salesman," Brandon explained. "He used to travel around a lot, and he kept his catalogues and stuff in that briefcase!"

"Are you sure?" Marlon asked.

"Yes! I used to climb into the briefcase when I was really little and ask my dad to take me with him. When I was older he let me help him pack. I *know* it's the same one."

Marlon took a step toward the young man, his eyes feverish. "I need you to think back, Brandon. How could this briefcase have ended up on your uncle's boat?"

Brandon stared up at the sky, biting his lip as he fought to remember. "I dunno. One day I guess it just wasn't around anymore. I thought my mom must have gotten rid of it so she wouldn't be reminded of him. And she probably thought I did the same thing. But Uncle Jack must have taken it. He spent the night at our place a few times after dad died. Helping out and stuff."

Marlon nodded. "Are there any markings on the briefcase? Anything that can prove it belonged to your father?"

"Yeah," Brandon said confidently. "His initials were inscribed on the lid. CTW. Christopher Theodore Watson."

Marlon turned to Sheriff Lustbader. "We need something long, skinny and rigid."

Five minutes later, having borrowed a broomstick from Donald Parks, Jasmine and Marlon were back on the boat. Using the same protocol as before, she was able to stick the broomstick into the cabin and record with her other hand. With some trial and error, she at last succeeded in closing the lid of the briefcase.

"Now make sure you get a good image," Marlon advised. "Be patient."

Jasmine gritted her teeth and ignored the burning in her shoulder as she stretched her arm around the tight corner, aiming in what she thought was the right direction.

In the end, they were able to confirm what Brandon said. The briefcase was inscribed with the initials CTW in large, gold letters. It was no wonder the thief of the money had not wanted the briefcase itself. It would have been a dead giveaway.

CHAPTER 12

"**G**loves on," Marlon said. "Booties, too."

Jasmine looked down. Her shoes were covered in ridiculous looking coverings, like face masks for your feet. She was also wearing a cheap, one-time-use plastic set of coveralls from the local hardware store, along with a set of kitchen gloves.

They were about to search Jack Torres's cottage, and this time Luffy was not allowed to enter. For consolation, he had been given a smoked pig's ear to chew at while he wallowed in his loneliness and misery on the front walk of the cottage.

"If you have to touch anything, photograph it in its original position first," Marlon said. "Above all, use common sense. And if you have any questions, feel free to ask me. I want this done right."

"Yes, sir," Sheriff Lustbader said. He looked rather ridiculous in his white plastic hazmat suit.

Marlon went through the door first, using a stone from just outside to prop it open. He flicked on the main light in the cottage, bringing the interior into view.

The air was stuffy and stale. Dust soon floated all around as the feet of the searchers disturbed it from the floor. The place was a mess; the cottage was all one room, apart from a tiny partition for the lavatory, and it was stacked and jammed full of random items.

"I guess Jack Torres was a bit of a hoarder," Marlon said. "This could be tough. Evidence is easy to miss in an environment like this."

Lustbader and the other deputies lingered just over the threshold, staring around like they had no idea where to start. But Jasmine charged forward, turning to sidle through a narrow corridor made of bookshelves overflowing with knickknacks. Suddenly, the rest of the world and the people within it were drowned out. She felt like she was alone in a universe of her own making, where she knew everything, and was in *control* of everything.

Something was drawing her onward. Pulling her through the cramped cottage. She let it happen, following along with this strange whim, glancing at things around her but not really seeing anything.

"Jasmine," Marlon called. "Moore, get back here! We need to do this systematically."

She ignored him. If he wanted to catch her, he would need to move fast. And she knew he wouldn't dare; there was too great a risk of knocking things over.

The bathroom door was open. She stepped inside, ducking her head instinctively under the low ceiling. There was a toilet, a sink, and a bath tub all packed into a room the size of her kitchen pantry. There was barely room to turn in a circle.

"Okay, now what?" she asked aloud.

The toilet lid was up. There was nothing inside but still, clear water. At least Crazy Jack kept his bathroom clean. *Very* clean, she suddenly noticed. Strangely clean, in fact. The floor was sparkling, each tile reflecting the light like little mirrors. The grout lines between them were fresh and white as though they'd just been laid a few days ago. There was a clean smell to the place, too. An unmistakable tang of bleach and scouring powder.

Jasmine turned to the sink, and found the same story there. Everything perfectly clean. There was a soap pump there. A tube of toothpaste. And Jack's toothbrush. Something about the brush stuck in her mind, and she couldn't stop staring at it for a few moments until she realized what it was.

The toothbrush was filthy. It would have scared any decent dentist half to death. It was so old that the brand etching on the handle had rubbed off. The bristles were flattened and brown with accumulated grime. Maybe, she thought, the brush had been used not to clean teeth but to clean grout lines. To try and confirm this, she lifted the brush toward her nose and, after psyching herself up, took a sniff.

The smell was faint. The brush hadn't been used for a while. But it was certainly the scent of toothpaste, minty and cool.

Setting aside the disturbing filthiness of the brush itself, Jasmine turned her mind to the paradox it presented. A perfectly clean bathroom, clean to the point of obsession... but a horribly dirty toothbrush.

With her pinky, Jasmine pulled open the medicine cabinet. It was mostly empty. There was a bottle of aspirin, some multivitamins, and a tube of ointment. What got her attention was the state of the little shelves; they were dusty, caked with dirt. Similar to the toothbrush.

Someone stepped up to the threshold behind her. Jasmine shut the cabinet and saw Marlon in the mirror.

"Alright in here?" he asked. "I just wanted to make sure you were observing the rules."

"I am," she said. "I haven't moved anything."

Well, she *had* moved the toothbrush, but she made sure to put it back where it had been.

Marlon nodded and withdrew into the main room of the cottage to start searching somewhere else.

When he was gone, Jasmine turned to the last item in the bathroom. The tub. It too had obviously been cleaned. The molded plastic, though scratched and scuffed here and there from years of use, shone brilliantly in the light. At the upper edge however, around the lip of the tub, she saw a few sprinklings of bluish powder. It was scouring powder, the same thing her mom used to clean the kitchen sink occasionally.

She stared at that powder, imagining the whole process in her head. Wet the tub down, sprinkle the powder, scrub until your arm felt it was going to fall off...

Rinse... watch the blue-stained water filter down the drain...

Her eyes followed that imagined course, down the walls of the tub, along its bottom, and finally to the fine metal strainer that sat over the drain hole, to catch any hair or other bits of matter.

Something stood out to her. Something pink in color.

Jasmine leaned in closer, shining the flashlight Lustbader had given her into the drain. There it was again, that pink luster, like little flecks of mica that danced in the light. There was a grouping of small particles caught in the drain, teetering on the edge. A single, thin trickle of water would have been enough to send them away. Out to sea, where they would never be found.

Holding her breath, Jasmine took out her phone and took as good a picture as she could of the particles. But the pictures weren't enough. They were blurry and inconclusive. She went out into the main room and signaled Marlon.

He stopped what he was doing and came over. "Did you find something?"

Jasmine explained everything she had observed since entering the bathroom. He listened intently. When she was finished, he moved past her without another word. She stood behind him, watching and holding her breath, as he used a delicate pair of tweezers to gather up each of the particles and deposit them in a small plastic bag.

"There," he said, sealing the bag and holding it up for her to see. "They're all safe."

"Do you have any idea what they are?" Jasmine asked.

"Not yet. It could be paint, maybe. But there's no paint that color in this house. It must have come from somewhere else. Jack got them on his body and they were left in the tub, stuck to the side somewhere. The cleaning process must have dislodged them enough that they ended up in the drain."

"Probably," Jasmine said, disappointed.

"But everything is potentially crucial evidence," Marlon replied. "We'll bring this back to the station for analysis. I believe the Blackwood Cove Police Department does at least have an electron microscope. An outdated one, but I spoke with Dr. Reynolds on the phone and he claims it still works just fine. It won't be enough to identify the substance with a single glance, but we can use it to make comparisons. Good work, Jasmine. Now, I think if you stay in here much longer that dog of yours is liable to have a fit."

Jasmine laughed, feeling guilty. "Luffy and I haven't spent much time apart since I found him when I was fourteen. I'm honestly pretty worried about what will happen when I go off to college."

"You could claim him as an emotional support animal," Marlon suggested.

"Is an FBI agent advising me to defraud the system?" Jasmine asked with a smile.

"Are you telling me you *don't* need Luffy?" Marlon asked. "Because it seems to me like you two are inseparable."

She nodded, unable to argue against the truth.

"Isn't there anything else I can help with here?" she asked.

"You can help by going home and getting some rest. Eat something. Relax for a bit. I'll need you sharp in a few hours when I'm back at the station with, hopefully, a mountain of evidence to sort through."

She nodded. They shook hands, and Jasmine left the building. Luffy immediately ran over to her, his tail wagging fiercely.

"You're back!" he said. "You're finally back! I thought I'd never see you again!"

"Where's Brandon?" Jasmine asked.

"Brandon? Oh! He went to return Donald's broom. But that was a while ago. I think he may need a rescue at this point."

"Then let's go."

They headed up to the next cottage. When they rounded the corner, they found Brandon sitting on an old plastic chair with a mug of cocoa in his hands. Donald Parks was deep into the telling of some tale, which seemed to be quite epic in length and scope.

"Sorry to interrupt," Jasmine said, "but we need to get back to work, Mr. Parks. We can come visit you again soon."

Donald looked at her through his fogged eyes and smiled. "That would be wonderful, Jasmine. Bye, now."

She felt bad as she stole Brandon away, setting his unfinished cocoa on the table beside him. Donald was even more alone than ever now, without his crazy neighbor Jack around.

But she needed Brandon for something. There was no way she was going to go home and sit around for hours waiting for something to happen. Not when Marlon's time was limited and the case felt so close to being solved.

***

"Are you sure about this?" Brandon asked.

"Absolutely not," Jasmine replied. "But we need to do it."

They were back near the commons. A cold wind blew, causing the leafless branches of the old oak tree to click and clack together like a xylophone made out of bones. An icy, clammy fog had rolled in, driving all but a single diehard jogger out of the area. As well as Jasmine, Luffy and Brandon, who stood on the sidewalk and stared up at the huge house occupied by Eugene and Laura Carter.

Already they could see someone watching them from a downstairs window. An ornery looking older woman with a dusting wand in her hands. She looked ready to spit venom, but Jasmine hadn't come here to be turned away so easily.

Grabbing Brandon's hand, she marched up the front walk of the house and rang the bell.

After a few moments, an artificially sweet and friendly voice came over a PA system and asked, "Who is it?"

Jasmine pressed a small button on a grille near the door to reply. "This is Jasmine Moore. I'm here with my friend Brandon Watson. We need to talk to the mayor and his wife. It's very important."

"I'm afraid you'll need to make an appointment," the voice answered. "And unfortunately they have busy schedules for the next week."

"I don't care about that," said Jasmine. "If they won't speak to me I'll bring an FBI agent, and it'll get a lot more unpleasant than it needs to be. Either way, I'm getting in there and they're *going* to answer my questions. The only thing that's up in the air is whether you want to do it the easy way or the hard way."

There was silence for close to half a minute.

"One moment please," the maid said. "I'll need to run this by Mr. Carter."

They waited some more. Finally there was a faint buzzing sound, a click of a lock, and the door opened. Jasmine tensed up, expecting the putrid maid to start chastising her... but it was only Eugene Carter, the mayor of Blackwood Cove.

Jasmine hadn't seen the man since the night Lustbader gave his address, but he hadn't changed much. He was still the same jolly looking fellow with perfectly combed salt and pepper hair and an eternal glint in his eyes. He had a smile loaded and ready to go as soon as the door opened.

"Miss Moore!" he said. "Mr. Watson! It's very good to see the both of you. And of course Luffy the dog! Who can forget about old Luffy?"

"Old?" Luffy asked. "Look who's talking."

"Come in, come in," the Mayor continued, stepping back and waving an arm. "But be sure to take off your shoes. The floors have just been cleaned and Teresa would kill me if I let someone track dirt all over them."

"I don't doubt it," Jasmine said. She entered the main hall of the manor and looked around. It was as she expected. A high ceiling, an ornate chandelier, hardwood floors. She could hear faint music, classical piano, drifting from somewhere.

She and Brandon removed their shoes. As they were doing this, the maid swept in with a towel and thrust it at them.

"Wipe the mutt's paws," she said.

"I'm no mutt, lady," said Luffy. "And you're uglier than my back end."

Jasmine smiled as she crouched down and cleaned the dog's feet.

Eugene cleared his throat, patting his pockets as though

searching for something. "I'm afraid I don't have much time to talk. We'll need to make this quick."

"Fine," Jasmine said, standing up and tossing the towel in the corner, to Teresa's obvious chagrin. "But I'll need to talk to Laura as well."

"That can be arranged," said Eugene. "She's just upstairs getting ready for our dinner. We're driving to the next town to meet with some people."

"How nice," Jasmine said distantly.

"Please, follow me," Eugene said.

They trailed him up the steps in their socks, their feet whisking silently over the oak planks of the floor. They reached a landing and turned left up into a second level corridor. The music was louder now.

Soon they entered a sort of parlor room where a stereo was playing. At a nearby makeup table, lit up by a ring of light bulbs, sat Laura Carter. She was the only woman in the Cove who could hold a candle to Cynthia's beauty. Plastic surgery and a pampered life had allowed her face to defy gravity for decades; she barely looked older than she had when she and Eugene first married.

"Do we have guests?" she asked, staring at herself in the mirror as she applied mascara. "Do I have to remind you we have an important dinner to get to?"

"No, dear," said Eugene. "Jasmine and Brandon have promised to take up a minimum of our time."

"I didn't make any promise," Jasmine said. "Even if I had, what does it matter if I break it? It wouldn't be any worse than all the promises you two have broken. You swore to live modestly, and here you are in a house three times bigger than mine. You swore to never forget your origins, and now you lock yourself away and ignore the troubles of your fellow townspeople. We elected you, and you have the *nerve* to refuse an interview from Julie Barnes? I can't believe I had to make threats to get in here!"

This drew Laura's attention. She stared at Jasmine in the mirror, the expressionless mask of her face framing eyes that glowed with anger.

"And you, girl, dare to enter our home and insult us?" she asked.

"I'm just trying to hold you accountable," Jasmine said.

"Now, now," said Eugene, stepping between the two women. "There's no need to get nasty here. Not at all. Jasmine, I apologize that we've been... aloof lately."

"That's a good word for it," Jasmine said. She was vaguely aware that Brandon had shrunken himself into one corner of the room, hiding from the argument.

"*But*," Eugene went on, holding up a finger, "it's just a matter of unfortunate timing. It just so happens that Jack died right as Laura and I were starting to broker a deal we've been after for years. It's something that will benefit the Cove for decades to come, and revitalize the economy. It may even bring back enough people to fill all our empty homes."

"That doesn't cut it," said Jasmine. "You could have given Julie twenty minutes."

"I explained to Julie that I would give her two hours if she wanted," said Eugene, "but it would have to wait a little while. I suppose she didn't believe me. She thought it was a big conspiracy to hide away and wait for the death of Jack Torres to blow over."

"It's not blowing over any time soon," Jasmine said. "You need to face the music, Eugene."

Laura Carter spun around on her stool now, holding a small bottle of nail polish. "You had better watch your tongue, little girl. My husband may be an elected official, but that doesn't give anyone the right to abuse him."

"The girl's right, sweetie," Eugene said with a smile, holding up a hand to placate his wife. "I do need to get my head out of the sand, here. This has gone on too long. Jasmine, you can ask me whatever questions you like. I'll call Julie tomorrow morning and let her know she can do the same. I've been so caught up in building the future that I forgot to hold the present together. It was my mistake."

"Thank you," Jasmine said. "That's all I wanted to hear."

The Mayor sat down on a nearby chair and motioned for her to continue.

"What did you think of Jack Torres when he was alive?" Jasmine asked.

"Unfortunately," said Eugene, "due to a night of debauchery at the Leaky Trawler, the town is well aware of how I felt about Jack. He was the one standout in a population of peaceful people. Crazy Jack was always there to mess things up and destroy the calm and quiet you're supposed to get in a small town like this. But now I'm struck by a great irony... Jack's dead, the black sheep is gone, and yet the town feels less safe than it did before. Lustbader's initial claim that Jack drowned accidentally isn't holding water with many people, I don't think. They may pretend to believe it to keep the peace in their own minds, but deep down they all suspect something else happened."

From the corner of her eye, Jasmine watched as Laura Carter calmly began to paint her nails, blowing on each one to dry the polish faster.

"What do you suspect?" Jasmine asked.

Eugene chuckled. "I suspect everyone's starting at phantoms. Wild ideas. Nothing more. People say Jack's the last person that could have drowned. Well, maybe that's true. But the guy they fished out of the water that morning was *not* Jack Torres. He was some shell of Jack, a leftover husk, burned out on the inside. Sick and crazed. If you ask me, Jack Torres died years ago. His body just didn't catch up for a while."

Eugene shook his head, staring at something far away.

"I wish things had gone differently," he continued. "When something like this happens, it makes me feel like I've failed as Mayor. And now I feel like I've failed all over again. This isn't who I am, Jasmine. And this isn't who *we* are, as a collective people. We help each other. We *forgive* each other."

"Tell this guy to save the speech for his reelection campaign," Luffy said. "We want real information here."

Jasmine barely heard. She was staring into space, toward

Laura. Suddenly she had forgotten everything she wanted to ask the Carters. Her mind was a blank, and she felt a strange panic rising inside her.

She stood up, and reached out her hand. "Thanks for your time, Mr. Carter. That's all I need for the moment."

The Mayor stared at her in surprise for a second, then smiled and shook her hand.

"Any time," he returned. "I mean that, now."

Jasmine gave Laura a nod and turned to leave the room.

"Laura smelled familiar," Luffy said quietly as they walked along the hall. "Real familiar. And I don't like that smell at all."

Jasmine wanted to ask him what he meant, but it would have to wait until later.

When they were out on the sidewalk again, Brandon finally broke his silence.

"What the heck are you *doing*?" he asked. "You wanted to get in there so bad, and you only asked, like, two questions!"

"I have everything I need for now," Jasmine replied, embarrassed about how her mind had shut down. "I set the Mayor straight. Hopefully he'll stop being such an idiot from here on."

"So, now what?" Brandon asked. "We just wait around for someone else to solve my Uncle's murder?"

She shook her head. "No. We go sit down at the Spyglass, have something to eat, and wait for either Lustbader or Marlon to call us."

***

The call came when they were halfway through their cherry pie. They immediately stood up, tossed some cash on the table, and hurried out of the diner. The police station wasn't far away; they jogged the entire way and came through the doors out of breath and burping up burgers.

"They're in the conference room," the receptionist said without looking up from her work.

They headed inside. Dr. Reynolds was there, back in action with an annoyed expression on his face. Lustbader was sitting down with a forgotten cup of coffee in front of him, and Marlon Gale was standing at the projector. He had connected a laptop to it, and was showing some photographs he had taken on the boat.

"Right on time," Lustbader said when the door shut behind Jasmine and company. "Agent Gale was just about to crack the whole case wide open."

"I wish," Marlon said. "But I did find a few things that might be important. First of all, during our second foray onto the deck of Jack's fishing boat, I saw these. Gouges that had been scratched into the deck, about three and a half feet apart. They were relatively fresh, too. The salt barely had time to seep into them."

"Which means," Dr. Reynolds said quickly, "they must have appeared on the most recent occasion on which the boat was used. The night of Jack's death."

"Exactly," said Marlon. "I don't know what made these scratches for certain, but I have some ideas. As soon as I find out, you'll all know too."

"Is there anything else?" Lustbader asked.

"Not much. We all know about the briefcase which belonged to Brandon's father."

"Yes," said Dr. Reynolds. "Brandon Watson, the boy who is most certainly *not* a deputy but for some reason is allowed to attend this meeting."

Marlon smiled at that. "I've had a growing feeling for the past two hours. If the feeling is right, all of this information will become publicly available anyway."

"You think you're about to solve it," said Dr. Reynolds in disbelief. "After scouring a messy cottage for three hours and coming up with nothing, you suddenly find yourself overflowing with confidence. Why?"

"Finger on the pulse," Marlon replied. "So, we all know about the briefcase and the money. And we all know about the pink particulate found in the bathtub drain. Apart from that, I'm afraid we have little to no evidence of any kind. Not at Jack's house, and not on his boat."

Dr. Reynolds clapped a few times. "Bravo. Now I understand

your certainty, Agent Gale."

"Don't get sarcastic just yet," Marlon said. "I have one more thing to look at. A little while ago I was able to look at the initial reports taken by the Blackwood Cove PD when Jack's body was discovered. I also found a piece of potential evidence that wasn't even tested."

Everyone looked at Lustbader.

"What?" he asked. "We thought the guy's death was an accident. At least we had the presence of mind to save *something*."

"It still might be an accident, Sheriff," Marlon said. "But we're about to find out together. Come with me, everyone."

He led them out of the conference room and down the hall to a room labeled EVIDENCE STORAGE AND ANALYSIS. Inside, he had already prepped what looked like a middle school science experiment. Three shallow dishes had been laid out, along with three nearly identical sealed beakers full of water. There was also a hair dryer that looked to have been liberated from the Cozy Cove Lodge.

"Come inside, gather 'round," said Marlon. "Look here, at these three beakers of water. One of them, this one on the far right, contains sea water that I collected a short while ago. The one here in the middle is filled with fresh water from the bathroom sink. And the one on the left is water that was collected from Jack's lungs during the initial inspection of the body."

Jasmine smiled. She saw where this was going.

"Now watch what happens," Marlon said.

He uncapped the beaker on the far right, the one with sea water. He poured a few drops into one of the shallow dishes, then turned the hair dryer on to the highest heat and aimed it at the water. It didn't take long for it to evaporate away.

Marlon shut the hair dryer off and lifted the now dry dish, rotating it in the light. It was clear to see that it was no longer clean; a cloudy, sparkling stain remained where the water had been.

"That's salt," Marlon said. "The water disappeared but the salt remained. Let's see what happens next."

He performed the trick again, this time pouring water from the vial of known fresh water into another dish. He hit it with the hair dryer until all the water was gone. This time, there wasn't much of a stain at all. Jasmine had to look very hard to see one. It was a faint smudge, nothing more.

"The tap water in Blackwood Cove isn't completely pure," Marlon said. "It's not like it's coming out of a distillery. This is a minor accumulation of minerals that you can find in most tap water across the country. As you can see, it's not anywhere near as drastic as the amount of salt left in the other dish."

Now he opened the last vial, the one with water taken from Jack's lungs. He repeated the procedure. Everyone watched, and Jasmine was certain she heard no one take a breath until the hair dryer switched off.

Marlon held the dish up. Jasmine saw nothing other than the same faint mist of minerals. Her mother would have called it a hard water stain.

"There are other tests that can be done," Marlon said, "but I think this is pretty conclusive. The water in Jack's lungs was *not* from the sea. He drowned somewhere else, in fresh water, and he was moved after his death. This does not prove murder, but it does highly suggest it."

Dr. Reynolds turned around and walked out.

CHAPTER 13

Without Dr. Reynolds around to wave the flag of procedure, the review of what little evidence they had went very quickly. Marlon had brought both the hundred-dollar bill and the briefcase from Jack's boat. After going over them for fingerprints, nothing usable was found.

"That's OK," he said. "We still might be able to get DNA off these things, once we send them to a better lab."

"Sorry, Agent Gale," Lustbader said, "but a mass spectrometer isn't exactly in the budget for a department like ours. Just count yourself lucky we have a coffee pot that works."

"I count myself very lucky, Sheriff," Marlon replied. "Usually I don't see this much cooperation and faith in my field work. Thanks for that."

Lustbader gestured at the table in front of them. "Go on, Agent. You've got one more thing to check out there."

It was the small plastic bag containing the pink particles Jasmine had found. She stared at them as Marlon carefully placed them in a slide and inserted it into a small microscope.

"Let's see here," Marlon said, pressing his eyes to the eyepiece. "It's been a while since I used one this small... Just have to get the right focus..."

"Wait," Jasmine said, feeling a strike of inspiration like lightning through her body.

Marlon leaned back to look at her.

"Let me see," she said.

He stood up, offering the chair to her.

She slid into place. But rather than look through the microscope eyepiece, she pulled out the slide and held it up to the overhead light.

"You have good eyes, Jasmine," Luffy said. "But I don't think they're *that* good."

"Wanna bet?" she asked.

All the humans in the room stared at her strangely. But she was barely aware of the slip she had made.

"I've seen this," she said, staring into the pink particles. "I'm sure of it."

"Where?" Marlon asked.

"When?" Lustbader added at almost the same time, their voices overlapping.

"Just a little while ago," Jasmine said with a growing smile. "In the mayor's house."

"*What?*" Brandon asked. "Jaz, I was there too and I didn't see anything like this!"

"You two were at the Carter residence?" Marlon asked, blinking in surprise.

Jasmine nodded. "While we were there, talking to Eugene, his wife Laura started painting her nails. She was painting them *pink*. This is the same exact shade and everything, Agent Gale. I just know it."

"I believe you," said Marlon. "But knowing is only half the battle. We have to prove it. You didn't happen to swipe her bottle of nail polish, did you?

"I'll pretend I didn't hear that," Lustbader said.

"Unfortunately not," Jasmine replied to Marlon's question. "We were there, talking, and suddenly my mind just went blank. Like someone wiped the slate. I thought at the time I was just tired, or nervous or something... but it was the nail polish! I was staring straight at it, but I didn't connect the dots until now. I saw the polish when she put it on wet, and I saw it when it was dry and hard. It's the *same*."

Marlon took the slide from her, setting it back in the

microscope carefully. "Then we'll need more. A larger sample size will help us make a positive match so we can move on this sooner. We'll need to go back to Jack's place and look more closely. At floors, at corners... we can even take the trap out of the bathroom sink drain and check in there."

**

Night had fallen by the time they exited the station. They took two cars. Jasmine and the Sheriff and Luffy rode in one, Marlon and Brandon in the other.

As their car followed the red taillights of the other through town, Lustbader gave Jasmine an appraising glance.

"When I wrote that note out for you," he said, "I didn't think a time would come when I'd be driving to a crime scene with you in my passenger seat. Not to mention your dog in the back."

"People surprise you sometimes," Jasmine said.

"Yep. They sure do. How did you manage all this, Jaz? How did you figure all this stuff out?"

She smiled to herself, thinking of Luffy and the visions that had been coming to her.

"You wouldn't believe me," she replied.

Lustbader shrugged. "As long as we don't find out you were an accomplice in the whole thing, I guess it doesn't matter. All that matters is that we figure this thing out. Together."

Luffy stuck his head into the front seat to give the Sheriff a big kiss on the cheek.

"Hey, I'm driving here!" the Sheriff said, gently pressing on the brakes.

They coasted into a red light on Main Street. A couple of people on their way out of the Spyglass Diner passed in front of them, going through the crosswalk. Lustbader waved at them. Meanwhile the first car in their convoy, carrying Marlon and Brandon, vanished from sight on the other side of the intersection.

"We'll catch up," Lustbader said, drumming on the steering wheel.

Jasmine sat back, feeling relaxed. Feeling safe. The heating vents in the car roared with warm air, driving the November chill out of her.

As they sat waiting patiently for the light to change, the Sheriff's phone rang. Before he could answer it, the light went green and he had no choice but to accelerate forward. The phone rang on for a few moments and finally died.

"Care to see who it was?" Lustbader asked.

Jasmine picked up the phone from the cup holder and looked at the missed call.

"It was from Donald Parks," she said.

"Huh. Must have thought of something else he wants to tell me. We can go check in with him once we get out there."

Onward they drove. They no longer saw the other car ahead of them, but the Cove was a small place. It couldn't have gone far.

They finally caught up with it in Bristol Lane, pulling in behind it at the curb. But the car was dark, empty, and Marlon and Brandon were nowhere to be seen.

"I guess we were at that light for a long time," Lustbader observed as he killed the engine.

They stepped out into the night air, breath pluming from their mouths. Jasmine opened the back door and Luffy came springing out, eager to join the adventure. The three of them walked up Bristol a ways, then cut down the familiar sandy path. As they were walking along, close to passing Donald's cottage on one side, they heard a voice hissing at them from somewhere up ahead.

"*Watch it!*"

Lustbader immediately fell into a crouch, pulling Jasmine with him. His other hand went to his sidearm and sat there at the ready.

Out of the darkness, waddling along in a squatting position, came Marlon Gale.

"What's going on?" Lustbader asked.

"Someone beat us to the cottage," Marlon said.

"Where's Brandon?" said Jasmine.

"Down the path a ways. He was ahead of me. Don't worry, he

saw it too. He's hunkered down somewhere."

Lustbader swallowed loud enough for Jasmine to hear. "What do we do, Agent?"

"Let me worry about that for now," said Marlon. "The two of you stay at my back. Sheriff, if whoever's in that cottage manages to get past me, you're the next line of defense. Make sure they don't get away."

"Okay," Lustbader said, taking a deep breath.

Marlon nodded. "Stay low."

He turned around and led the way. Jasmine and Luffy took up the rear, shuffling along.

The sky was clear. Brilliant moonlight shone down upon Blackwood Cove, turning the night to some ethereal ghost of its usual self. Jasmine felt like she was in a dream as she made her way down that path. As they passed Donald's cottage, she glanced over and saw him staring out the window at her with a look of concern on his face. It was soon replaced by relief when he realized that he was not actually looking at four giant crabs but rather at the cavalry he had attempted to call in.

"I don't know if I can do it," Lustbader said.

"Do what?" Marlon whispered back.

"Use my gun. I've never fired it except at the range."

"All you have to do is hold it out and use a loud voice," Marlon replied. "We don't want to use lethal force here, anyway. The idea is to take the person into custody."

Lustbader breathed a sigh of relief.

As they neared the end of the path, Marlon and Lustbader split off for Jack's cottage. The agent signaled for Jasmine to hang back, and so she crept to the side, positioning herself in the tall scrub grass.

From there, she stared over at the cottage. It was dark. No lights burned inside. But in the glow of the moon she saw that the door was hanging open, a yawning mouth ready to swallow Agent Gale whole.

Something moved to Jasmine's right. A rustle in the grass. She gasped and looked over... but it was only Brandon, sneaking toward her. For a moment her head spun, reality painted over in the strange colors of déjà vu. But it was a feeling she was starting to get used to.

"Jaz, is that you?" Brandon whispered.

"Yeah," she replied.

The grass rustled again as he continued toward her. They huddled together, Luffy between them, and watched.

Lustbader's gun was drawn. He was crouched on the path, ready and waiting. Ahead of him, Agent Marlon Gale was just climbing the steps into the darkened cottage. In a second he was gone, swallowed up in shadow.

Jasmine held her breath.

There was a shout. A crashing sound, followed by several bangs and thuds. Lustbader jumped to his feet, extending his trembling arms to train his weapon on the door.

Someone came running out, tripping over a scattering of books and other debris. They went head over heels, crashing down onto the front walk, then rolling up onto their feet. As soon as they saw Lustbader, they froze still.

In the moonlight, the identity of the person was plain. Even though she was wearing baggy clothes that were dark to blend in with the night.

It was Laura Carter.

"*Stop!*" came a roar from inside the cottage. "*Lustbader, stop her!*"

"Um... hold it right there," Lustbader shouted. "I mean it, Mrs. Carter. Don't you-"

Laura turned abruptly to the side, dashing across the sand. Lustbader tracked her with his weapon, but did not fire. In a second she had vanished from his sight behind the building.

At last Marlon emerged from the cottage, rubbing his head as though he'd been struck by something.

"Let's go!" he said. "After her!"

Lustbader shook himself out of his funk and the two men began to run.

Jasmine stood up in the grass and followed behind them.

Luffy cried out, whining in terror, but finally he relented and rushed to join her.

In the night, Jasmine ran down the beach, following three dark figures. One was far ahead of the others; Laura was headed straight for the docks where her yacht was tied off.

She wouldn't be able to escape on *that*, Jasmine thought. There was no way. Taking off in a yacht was not a speedy affair. What was the woman doing?

Huffing in the cold air, digging deep for an extra burst of energy, Jasmine lurched forward and soon passed Sheriff Lustbader. But Marlon was still gaining speed, his legs and arms a blur as he sprinted after the mayor's wife.

Laura Carter hopped up the stairs, mounting them two at a time. The night filled with a hammering sound as she ran along the loose wooden boards.

"*Stop!*" Marlon cried out.

Five seconds behind her, Marlon climbed onto the docks as well.

Jasmine went off on her own course. She moved right, splashing out into the water, avoiding the dock's main stairs and cutting a few seconds off her travel time. She leapt up and grabbed onto the side of the platform, climbing up into that moonlit world of boats bobbing in the waves, of wooden pylons squeaking quietly in the surf as they shifted ever so slightly.

She hauled Luffy out of the water and set him beside her.

"Go get her," she said.

Luffy took off without a word, charging up the dock. He soon passed Marlon, gaining ground on Laura at an astonishing rate.

The mayor's wife looked back, terror widening her eyes.

But she wasn't going for her yacht. Not anymore, at least. It was too far out, parked at the very end of the docks. And of course she knew better than anyone how long it would take to get the boat moving.

Instead, she darted to the side. Toward a spot on the docks that was familiar to everyone in town, because it was a spot no one had been able to use for many years.

Laura leapt into space. She seemed to hang there for a moment, suspended in the moonlight. And then she fell, landing in the old, mossy canoe that had been tied there for as long as Jasmine had been alive.

There was a sound of splintering wood, followed by a mighty splash as Laura fell straight through the canoe and into the water.

Luffy drew up short, standing on the edge of the dock and barking at her.

"Where do you think you're going?" Marlon shouted, stumbling to a stop on the rickety platform. He holstered his weapon and fell to his knees, beckoning. "Come on. Get out of that water. You'll freeze to death."

Laura gasped with the cold as she paddled over and grabbed onto his hand. He pulled her up to safety and wrapped his own jacket around her.

By that time, Lustbader had finally caught up. He pulled a pair of handcuffs off his belt and slapped them on Laura's wrists.

"I guess you already know this," he said, "but you're under arrest. You have the right to remain silent..."

He continued to Mirandize her as he led her off the docks. But Jasmine didn't hear it. She was too busy staring at the wooden platform, at the wet footprints that Laura left behind.

CHAPTER 14

"It was all pretty simple once we put the pieces together," Jasmine said. "There aren't many things Luffy growls at. He's a very relaxed dog."

He looked up at her. "Yup. Yes I am. Friendly dogs get the most treats."

"But he didn't like Laura's smell," Jasmine went on. "He hated it."

Julie typed all of this down on her keyboard, though she couldn't possibly know why it was relevant just yet.

"Laura's a smart woman," Jasmine said. "After she killed Jack, she never felt safe. She was always looking over her shoulder, paranoid... When she saw me leaving the address that night, on the commons, and heading toward the police station, she knew something was up. So she followed me through the fog, and she followed me home too, staying out of sight, listening and watching. I thought Luffy was growling at Brandon, but he was actually growling at *her*. He knew she was there."

"I didn't really know," Luffy added. "I just knew I smelled something rotten."

"Laura knew I was going to be digging around, so she got cautious. She found a way for her and her husband to withdraw from the public eye. Lay low for a while. And when we finally visited the Carter house, Laura's vigilance almost paid off again. Maybe she saw me staring at her nail polish and it got her thinking. That night, she stole down to Jack's cottage to see if she had missed something."

"Had she?" Julie asked.

"Yes, but we had already found it. Traces of her nail polish in the bathtub. It didn't take very long for Marlon to make a positive match."

Julie nodded. "So how did it all happen? How did Laura do it?"

"She was at the Leaky Trawler the night Jack died. Or she was nearby. All I know is, she knew how drunk he was. How vulnerable. She went to his cottage, and I suppose she must have found him getting ready for a bath. She held his head under water, and she drowned him. Once he was dead, she knew she had all night to set the scene right. So she took her time. She dragged him out onto his boat. And then she took her jet ski, the one tied up beside her yacht, and brought that onboard as well. We know it was there, because we matched it with gouges found on the deck.

"She took his boat out a ways and dumped his body into the water. Then she abandoned ship, taking her jet ski back to shore. She went slow, trying to avoid attracting any attention. Brandon was on the beach that night, wandering around. He heard a motor out in the water... I think it must have been Laura. When she got back to land, she returned to Jack's cottage and got busy. She spent most of her time in the bathroom, cleaning it until it shined. She scrubbed out the bathtub as well. She would have used a rough sponge and scouring powder. At some point she chipped her nail polish, and some of it ended up sticking to the strainer."

"And that's what sealed it," said Julie.

Jasmine nodded. "If it wasn't for that, we wouldn't have gone back to the cottage that night. We wouldn't have been able to catch her so easily. But the particles might have been enough for a search warrant, Marlon tells me. We would have found the truth sooner or later."

"So, you really did crack the case, Jasmine," Julie said with a smile.

"With a lot of help from my friends, bipedal and otherwise," said Jasmine.

Julie typed for a minute, catching up.

"So we have the *how*," she said. "That can be described in great detail. But what I don't know is the *why*. There seems to be no motive at all."

"There is one," Jasmine promised. "But I don't have all the information. I'm just a girl from Blackwood Cove who helped solve a murder. I don't have a lot of authority. But here's what I *do* know. Agent Gale and the FBI are working closely with other government law enforcement agencies on the matter. Laura and Jack were only the beginning of something larger. A criminal enterprise that plies its trade off the New England coast. It seems like Jack was something of a middleman. Laura was higher up, benefitting from his work. Something went wrong. There was a disagreement over payment... Whatever the case, it was all about money."

"Why did Jack try to frame Randy Ballard?" Julie asked.

"Because he was an easy target. Jack wanted a backup. A trump card, in case law enforcement started sniffing around his cottage. So he drummed up all this nonsense about Randy, so he could whip it out at the right time and say 'I told you so.' He thought it could distract the cops long enough for him to get away."

"That's crazy," Julie said, shaking her head.

"They did call him Crazy Jack. And it's the truth."

"It's a giant mess, is what it is. Blackwood Cove, site of murder and now a criminal organization! I think this next season is going to be dubbed the Year Without Tourists. It's going to kill us."

Jasmine shrugged. "I don't know about that. People love a scandal. Besides, we're making history. This is the first significant thing to happen in our town since..."

"Since I don't even want to know when," Julie groaned. "Well, thank you for keeping your word. I already have online orders from all over the country, asking for the next issue. This is going to be a big story. Are you bothered by that?"

Jasmine had given it a lot of thought. Maybe it wouldn't be so bad being a bit of a celebrity. When you were famous for solving a murder, it guaranteed that none would occur when you were around. That seemed like a good thing to her.

She shook her head. "No, I'm fine with it. I'm happy for you, Julie."

The editor grinned and stood up. The two of them hugged.

"And I'm happy for *you*," Julie said. "Getting into Wildwood University? That's quite an accomplishment! I heard they have one of the highest rejection rates in the country."

"The world, actually," Jasmine said. "It's not a big deal. It's just that they're so small. They don't have room for many people."

"Cut it out with the modesty! That won't serve you at all in the real world. You need to be proud of yourself and what you've done. Leave it to the rest of humanity to downplay your achievements. Because they always will. Just make sure you don't let it get to you."

Jasmine reached down, rubbing Luffy's head. "Don't worry, Julie. I'll stay strong. I have the benefit of bringing my best friend with me."

They said goodbye to the editor of the Cove Herald, and stepped out into town. A cold wind blew out of the commons, carrying with it a tide of autumn leaves that rustled underfoot.

"On to the next adventure, I guess," Luffy said.

"On to the next adventure," Jasmine agreed.

"I'm going to miss this place."

"Me too. But we aren't leaving yet. We still have to say goodbye to Patrick."

It was a short walk to The Book Nook. Instead of entering into the usual library-esque silence, they instantly heard the sound of animated conversation as they stepped through the doors.

Jasmine looked at the counter, where Brandon was sitting. He rolled his eyes at her and motioned toward the center of the store.

She followed the sounds of arguing and soon found Cynthia and Patrick, engaged in some sort of heated debate.

"The second book is obviously the best in the series!" Cynthia said.

Patrick sighed. "Please. It's just a rehash of everything that happened in book one. It's not until the third book that you'll find any original writing."

"You're dead wrong! Book one is the hero's journey, and book two is the hero's *fall.* It's a completely different plot device!"

Jasmine turned on her heel and returned to the counter, smiling as that sense of déjà vu washed over her again.

"The lovebirds are at it again," she said.

"Yeah, they've been at it a *lot* lately," Brandon said. "But the good news is, Patrick finally let me buy him a new computer. It should be getting here on Tuesday. But I guess..."

"I won't be here to see its beauty," Jasmine said.

He nodded. "Right. Off to college. I'm happy for you. I guess it paid off, huh? Waiting to get into the right school."

"You'll miss me," Jasmine said, grinning.

"Who says?"

"Says your sad little eyes. Don't worry, I'll be back in between semesters. You can't keep me away."

Brandon smiled. "I wouldn't try."

They had already said their goodbyes the day before. There was nothing left to be said that couldn't wait a few months, and the longer Jasmine stood around the less she would want to leave. So she and Luffy exited the Nook, leaving behind its stacks of treasures.

"*Now* it's on to the next adventure," Jasmine said. "So long, Blackwood Cove."

Luffy barked, an echoing call that bounced down the empty street, along the commons, and off the library building, echoing back to them. It was his own farewell.

Farewell, for now.

END OF BOOK 1

BOOK 2: When a promising young student plunges to his

death from a historic clock tower, Jasmine knows that foul play is involved. Once again summoning her detective skills and her faithful companion Luffy, she must solve another case and catch an evasive killer.

A Timely Murder is now on Amazon at https://www.amazon.com/gp/product/B08B33WVV5

FREE NOVELLA: A roaring blizzard. A rest area in the middle of nowhere. Seven strangers stranded with a dead body. The killer is close by, and no one's going anywhere. In *Cold Case*, there are secrets lurking in the snow.

Join Max Parrott's author newsletter and get *Cold* Case for FREE only at https://dl.bookfunnel.com/boa2a0o66q

Dear Reader,

Hope you have enjoyed the ride. If you have...
...could you kindly leave a review?

Thanks,
Max

P.S. Reviews are like giving a warm hug to your favorite author.

We love hugs.

https://www.amazon.com/dp/B088LJZM57

Printed in Great Britain
by Amazon